All ⌐

All Things New Again

Oceanside Inn Series

Morris Fenris

Published by Morris Fenris, 2022.

ALL THINGS NEW AGAIN

First edition. May 30, 2022.

Written by Morris Fenris.

Table of Contents

Morris Fenris

All Things New Again

Oceanside Inn Series Book Five

Prologue

Molly Hessinger was surprised when the door of her small office was flung open by a very eager looking Tanner, her assistant as head of the financial department at Oceanside Inn, where she worked.

Five years she'd been working at the Inn, only the last two as the head of the department. Tanner had been the assistant for the previous person in that position and told her on numerous occasions how glad he was that she was now his boss.

Even so, in all that time, she'd never seen him looking so excited.

"Tanner!" she exclaimed. "What's got you all excited?"

"Steven wants to see you. I think the rumors are true!"

He looked gleeful and Molly had to admit, underneath it all, she was fairly happy about the rumored changes she'd heard coming as well. Steven Smith, her good friend and the owner of Oceanside Inn was said to be bringing in some new blood, revitalizing the online presence of the Inn. At present, there was very little, which was shocking considering how important it was to be online these days.

The thought of having a web department at the Inn made Molly apprehensive, but eager to see what could be created. She'd been fascinated by the details of creating websites since she was first introduced to it at the age of twelve. She quickly learned HTML and other common web languages. For a while, she thought about going into that field but decided working with numbers was better for her, so she became an accountant.

When she started at the Inn five years ago, Molly was put in charge of the accounting department. She learned over the years and her suggestions for restructuring found her at odds with the head of finance at the time.

Steven agreed with her vision and had to dismiss the head of finance, but the man was given an extensive severance package. He put Molly in the man's place and she'd been thriving ever since. Because of her guidance, the Inn was now close to the success it had once been. They had regular visitors, the boats were all in fine shape, no parts of the Inn were shut down due to maintenance concerns, the restaurants were lauded in local and nationwide magazines and newspapers.

She'd found she had a knack not just for numbers, but also for advertisement and marketing.

She stood up, glancing down at the papers she'd been going over.

"You will come right back and let us know if the rumors are true, won't you?" Tanner asked.

"Of course. I better get to his office." She was speaking under her breath as she passed him, her mind on the task of restructuring once again if a new department was going to be added. She'd seen no new offices being built, and no equipment had come in.

Maybe that's what Steven was about to talk to her about.

She nodded at Tanner as she hurried from the room, going down the long hallway to the end and pushing the door open to let her out into the concourse where his office was at.

There were guests all around the room, murmuring to each other as they gazed admiringly at the large framed photos of historical places all around Virginia that hung on the walls, along with the other decorations displayed for their enjoyment.

Steven had a new secretary, a bubbly redhead named Candy, appropriately enough, and she smiled brightly as Molly approached.

"Go on in, Molly," she said. "He's expecting you."

"Thanks, Candy."

She turned her feet toward the door to Steven's office, but her eyes trailed slowly across the row of seats just behind Candy's desk. One of the chairs was occupied. The man was looking down at his phone, which he was holding in one hand.

Her eyes lingered on him a little longer than they normally would on a stranger. Was he the new employee? Was the media department going to consist of him and him alone?

She moved her eyes to the door in front of her, thinking he was dressed for a new job. He had on a nice dark blue blazer and blue slacks and his black shoes looked newly polished.

She couldn't see his face or really gather any other information about him based on sight. But his presence gave her a bit of a thrill. She was ready for a change. Things had been incredibly boring around the Inn lately, as things had been running like clockwork.

She tapped on the door lightly before turning the knob and stepping in. Steven looked up as she entered, smiling wide. He held out one hand to the comfortable chair on the other side of his desk.

"Have a seat, Molly."

Molly glanced at the other chair that had been pulled up closer in front of his desk. Usually it was just the one.

"Tanner said you wanted to see me."

Steven nodded, leaning forward, his elbows on the desk and his hands in front of him, fingers laced together. "I'll get right to the point. I know you've heard the rumors of a new media department coming to the Inn. Those rumors are true. I didn't want to say anything about it until I found the right person for the job. He's outside, and I told Diana to wait ten minutes before sending him in after you got here."

Molly grinned at her friend. "Candy."

Steven blinked at her.

"You said Diana," she clarified. "The girl's name is Candy. I sure hope you aren't calling her that to her face."

Steven chuckled, shaking his head. "I can't get used to Di not being here," he said. "Anyway, yes, I told Candy that. I wanted to talk to you first and see if you had any questions."

Molly chuckled. "I have no questions yet, but I might later on. I'm anxious to meet this man. Is he going to be the whole department all by himself?"

"Heh, heh, that sounds like a question," was his response. He winked and continued. "No, he's the tip of the iceberg. I've given him permission to check out the duties and the property and offices and report back to let me know what he needs as far as equipment and personnel."

"Well, let's have him in," Molly said, anxiously.

Chapter One

Molly stood up when Steven went around his desk to get the man from the hallway. She didn't realize he hadn't told her what to call the man until he said a name out loud and gestured.

"Eddie. Come on in."

He continued as Eddie came in but Molly barely heard what he was saying. When he walked in, her heart did an unexpected leap. Molly was sure he couldn't be more than a few inches taller than her. Her immediate thought was that he reminded her of a teddy bear.

"Eddie Button," Steven said, gesturing between the two of them. "Molly Hessinger. Molly, this is Eddie, the media man."

Molly saw Eddie's side glance of amusement to Steven as he came toward her, holding out his hand.

"It's good to meet you, Molly," he said.

Molly's worst fear was about to happen. She could tell already. She opened her mouth, forcing herself to stay calm as she shook his hand. "Likewise," she said in a surprisingly calm voice, considering the way her heart was doing somersaults in her chest. "I haven't really heard much about you. I've been hoping for a media department, though. I've been handling it all on my own."

Molly was extremely proud of herself for concealing the immediate attraction she felt for the man in front of her. Eddie Button. What a name. It fit him, at least physically. He was short, like her, couldn't be more than five foot six. He was on the softer side, not fat or plump. He wasn't teeming with muscle and oozing masculinity. His wavy brown hair looked soft enough to run one's fingers through.

Molly didn't want her thoughts to run away with her.

But when she looked into his hazel eyes, she felt like she couldn't breathe for a moment. She forced herself to resume her seat, dragging her gaze away from him and placing it back on Steven's face as he sat behind his desk. She studied him, wondering if he could tell what she was feeling. They'd been friends through high school and college, which was one of the reasons she'd been offered the job here at the Inn.

He was tapping papers on his desk so they were even with each other.

"I have all the documents you'll need to sign to start today right here," he said, flipping the pages over so they were held out to Eddie, who took them. "You can sign them at your leisure. Obviously you'll be paid for coming in today and working. You can leave whenever you want. But that's just for today. Don't go taking advantage of it." He said the words with a grin so Eddie would know he was joking.

"You mentioned I'll be shadowing for a lot of today," Eddie said. "I'm assuming that's so I can see what…" He glanced at Molly, which made her heart thump hard in her chest. "Molly has been doing so far?"

"Yes, that's exactly what you'll be doing today," Steven replied with a nod. "Any questions you might have should be directed to her. Any problems, too."

"And suggestions," Molly spoke up, attempting to sound professional and helpful. "I can relay them to Steven even if you do put them in your report. You know, to show my support."

Eddie scooted forward in his chair so he could use the desk in front of him to sign the papers. "I'm just gonna sign these now and get it over with," he said, lifting his eyes to Steven from the paper. "You don't mind, do you?"

"No, not at all. There's five of them there. You'll want to sign..."

Molly stopped listening to their conversation. While he discussed the documents with Steven, she examined the new employee. How could she be expected to work with someone she was so immediately and so intensely attracted to? She'd never believed in love at first sight. It seemed a ridiculous notion to her.

She had never married, and at almost forty, Molly hadn't been interested in a man for nearly a decade. It wasn't for lack of looking. She just wasn't concentrated on it. She figured when God wanted to send a man her way, He would. And He would likely make it obvious because Molly had found herself to be pretty clueless in that department over the years.

She felt a tingle inside. Had God sent her a man?

Was it finally her time?

Molly had to scold herself silently. She couldn't let her imagination run wild. She had known this man for five minutes and didn't know a thing about him. The instinctual pull she felt was probably just hormones. Maybe it had been too long since she went on a date.

Molly caught herself before she snorted out loud. Both men stopped talking and looked at her when she made the strange guttural noise and she pretended to cough, lifting one fist to her mouth and turning away from them.

"You all right?" Steven asked.

She glanced back, nodding, choking out another cough or two. "I'll be fine," she said. She couldn't believe she'd just made herself look like an idiot in front of the new guy. She wanted to crawl into a hole and die.

"Okay, so that's the plan and I look forward to reading your report." Steven stood up, holding out his hand. He continued to speak while they shook. "I'll get this paperwork over to HR for you. You need anything Molly can't provide, my door is always open. Oh, and don't hesitate to put on there whatever kind of equipment you need, computers and all that. I have a stash put aside for electronics and new technology. Thanks to this woman's mathematical genius, we are swimming in dollars."

"Might as well take advantage of that, right?" Eddie said with a grin.

"Yes."

Steven ushered the two of them out. Molly felt hot as she walked beside Eddie to the door to her department.

"Right down this way," she said, smiling at Eddie. This time, when she looked into his eyes, she saw something other than just how attractive he was. There was something deeper there. Molly would never pry. But she hoped that someday she would find out the reason for that intense look he carried. At first, she'd thought of him as a teddy bear. But looking into his eyes gave her the impression he might not be that cuddly, after all.

It wasn't something she would hold against him. She liked substance. She liked that he had a sharp brain. He had to for Steven to give him a job and free rein over the checkbook.

"You'll meet Tanner. He's my assistant. We don't have a lot of employees working for us. I'll be surprised if you get more than two or three employees for your department, once it's up and running." She pulled open the door and went through to the long hallway.

"That's fine," Eddie replied as he followed her. The door closed automatically behind him. "I'm not worried about that. I actually think I can handle the media stuff all on my own. Especially if I have you helping me. During my interview, Steven had a lot of good stuff to say about you. I was... I'll tell you I was impressed. I'm usually..." He wasn't looking at her when she glanced at him, "Usually not so open with people, but... you've got a nice face."

Molly's heart quaked.

"So does Steven," Eddie said, putting a damper on Molly's elation. "He's got a face people can just talk to like you do. It's nice to find that at a new job. Makes it easier to... well, to ease in, I guess, right?"

When he grinned at her, she hoped he didn't see how she really felt when she smiled back.

Chapter Two

As they walked down the hallway, Eddie marveled at the fact that he could come to a new place of employment and feel so comfortable, so fast. It was doubly shocking, because he typically wasn't someone who warmed up to other people easily.

Eddie was an orphan after the age of six, and placed with a foster family who lived on a farm in southern Virginia. They had many acres, lots of land for children to explore. The couple were older but still had enough energy to do and plan fun activities for the children they fostered, which, at one point, had been eight children besides Eddie.

Peter and Anna Lawler had been good foster parents. They didn't put the children "to work" other than general age-appropriate chores they were given. They fed and clothed the children, let them play, and taught them regularly. There was a large barn on the property they had transformed into an old time schoolhouse, and a teacher of all grades came in to teach the children on days when other children were in school.

The Lawlers let the children decide their futures. They raised them into adults and let them go. To Eddie, that was the best thing they could have done. He was raised with warmth, comfort, security, and sustenance.

But for some reason, of all the children the Lawlers took in over the years, Eddie was the one who fell through the cracks. Though he was present for the events, adventures, travels and fun the Lawlers organized for the children, he'd grown up feeling like he wasn't actually seen. He was just another child.

He received no one-on-one love from either Peter or Anna. They weren't mean to him. They just weren't *parents* to him. Anna was clearly not his mother. It was the same for Peter.

Eddie didn't know if he'd ever felt love for another person. The farm had given him a deep-rooted love for animals, though.

If he could have gotten away with working from home, he would have. There were no jobs, though, that he could do from home that would give him the kind of benefits and money the job at the Inn would provide. It was the best way, in his opinion, to ensure he had a future worth looking forward to. He already assumed he would be on his own. So that's what his life goal was based on.

Eddie went through another doorway behind Molly and was greeted by a young man in his twenties who looked bright and smiling and happy. He was taller than both of them.

Eddie wasn't as touchy about his height as he could have been. One thing Anna Lawler had taught him as he grew up and they realized he wasn't going to pass five foot six, was that his height didn't define what kind of man he was.

"Good things come in short packages," she used to say, "if I might paraphrase a common phrase."

That always made Peter laugh and the two of them would ruffle his hair and walk away. He couldn't remember either of them having spent more than five minutes alone with him.

Still, he had fond memories of them and frequently visited their graves. They'd passed within a few weeks of each other just after Eddie's thirty-sixth birthday three years ago. He'd been there with several of the other children they'd fostered—now grown adults, some with grandchildren of their own.

"Tanner, this is Eddie. He's going to be the new media department until he gets his own employees." Molly smiled at him. "Unless he decides not to get employees and just does it all himself."

Tanner raised one eyebrow, the same side of his lips lifting in a mischievous half grin. He was looking pointedly at Molly. "Oh, we don't know anyone else who does that, do we?"

Molly laughed and swatted at the young man. Eddie could see they had a pleasant and friendly working environment. No matter where he looked, he just kept seeing benefits to working at the Inn. It was practically a miracle that he'd gotten it in the first place.

"I'm not like that," Molly insisted, her voice lifting and falling musically. Eddie liked her very much. He could see they would be kindred spirits. Plus, he liked the way she looked at him. He'd never had a woman look at him quite like that before. She looked at him like he was a delicious drink she couldn't wait to try.

It made him feel tingly inside.

"Oh!" Tanner looked regretful, turning his wide eyes to Eddie. "I wasn't talking about her. No, I was talking about someone completely different from her."

Eddie appreciated their humor and gave them a smile. He wondered if they were putting on a show for him or if they were naturally like that. He had a feeling it was the latter. They didn't seem like the type of people who weren't secure with who they were to begin with.

"I didn't have much notice you were coming," Molly said as she went around the desk to her chair. Eddie turned just in time to see Tanner dragging a metal fold out chair with a thin cushion attached over to the desk, jerking it so the seat would fall open and dropped down on it dramatically. He wondered if the young man was always this excited to see a new person.

"Actually, I didn't have *any* notice," Molly continued, gesturing to the more comfortable cushioned chair directly in front of her desk. "So I thought, just now, as we were walking down the hallway, of course, that maybe we could sit down and get to know each other."

Eddie was once again surprised that he felt no resistance to that plan. He hated talking about himself. He was always lost for words. What could he really say? There wasn't much to him, other than that he was good with computers. He had no funny jokes to tell. He wasn't the "comedy relief" friend that a bunch of people seemed to have. He liked to read books and enjoyed a good mystery TV show. One of his favorite pastimes was reading books and then watching the TV or movie rendition of that book. It gave him the perfect opportunity to compare the two. He often wished he had someone to discuss those interests with.

It didn't occur to Eddie that what he had just been thinking about himself was, in fact, something he could tell his two new friends until he looked into Molly's eyes and she smiled at him.

"I'll start," she said, abruptly, as if she hadn't planned on it to begin with. "I'm Molly." She laughed softly, making Eddie's heart warm up. "I'm the head of the finance department here at Oceanside Inn." She looked up at the ceiling as if trying to remember something. When she dropped her eyes again, they sparkled in the overhead fluorescent light and made Eddie grit his teeth. For some reason, she seemed a lot prettier to him than she had just a few minutes ago.

He wasn't sure what was happening, but at least he was enjoying it.

"I..." She dragged out the word, letting her eyes wander around the room. "I, uh, love to work with numbers. When I was a kid, I would play number games all the time. When Soduko started getting popular, I was on that like white on rice. I love it. I... I've never been married. I went to college, with Steven I might add, and some of the other heads of departments here at the Inn. I've been working here for five years now, two as the head of the finance department, with Tanner here as my assistant."

"You were working here when she was made head of finance?" Eddie asked, moving his eyes to the young man.

Tanner nodded and then shook his head immediately afterward, closing his eyes momentarily. "If you are thinking what you're probably thinking, don't worry about me. I didn't want the job. I still don't. I love being an assistant, especially when the boss tells me I need to go get some coffee. You want some coffee or a drink or something?"

"I'd love a bottle of water if you've got some," Eddie replied, suddenly parched. Probably from his heart beating faster than normal.

Tanner nodded. "You got it. I'll be right back."

Chapter Three

The day went by too quickly for Eddie. The job had everything he wanted. Friendly people, an interesting proposal, things to think about and dwell upon while he went about his nightly routines. He was hoping it would be that way.

He'd made several lists during the day about what he needed to make the "media department" of the Inn a success. It had been some time since the website they had—which Eddie discovered Molly didn't even know existed—was updated. In fact, the website still had Steven's Uncle Ben as the owner and proprietor. The man had been dead for five years and no one saw fit to update the website.

After meeting Steven, Eddie understood better why the media had fallen to the wayside. It wasn't something he concentrated on. Eddie was willing to bet he didn't have a social media account at all.

He was probably better off without the social media. Eddie knew how to market online and would put his talents to good use quickly. The media would be updated every day, once he had it built. He didn't need anyone else working with him. He didn't need an assistant or anyone else to help him.

In fact, he was wondering what his job would be after he had the website built and the social media accounts updated. It would take him an hour to send updates in the morning. And what if there were no updates? Would Steven let him go once he saw he was paying a good deal of money for Eddie to post an advertisement on social media and then go out for a forty-five minute break?

Maybe with Molly beside him?

He grinned as he pulled his Toyota up the driveway to his house. He owned a brick ranch house on the outskirts of Vinton and would enjoy the commute of thirty-five minutes every morning.

Eddie pushed the door open and stepped inside, halting at the entrance. He looked to the left and to the right, anticipation making him smile.

"Hello?" he called out, as if he expected a wife and children. "I'm home. Anyone here?"

He took a few more steps in and looked around again, pretending not to see the brightly colored parrot perched on a swing in a golden cage attached to the ceiling in front of the kitchen bar window.

"Anyone here?" he said again.

"Hello, Eddie," Jackson, Jr., his best friend and proud member of the parrot kingdom, spoke up clearly.

Eddie turned to the bird, grinning wide. "Well, hello there, Jackson, Jr. What are you doing here? I thought you flew away!"

"Never fly away," the bird replied. "Never fly away."

"Good." Eddie reached through the bars of the cage and brushed one finger gently against the bird's beak and the side of his small head. Jackson Jr. rested his head to the side and closed his eyes, purring like a kitten. "I guess I'd be lost without you. So I started my new job today, you know."

"New job," Jackson Jr. replied.

"Yeah, I think I'm going to like it." He set his keys and wallet on the kitchen bar window and crossed his arms, leaning on them. "There's a lady working there..."

Jackson Jr. made a low whistling sound in his throat. Eddie imagined his bird friend was wiggling his eyebrows. He laughed.

"Now, now. She's a nice lady. She won't be my boss, but she will be a coworker. I can't be thinking about her like that. It's way too soon for anything like that."

Eddie didn't know what he was talking about. He suspected even his bird knew he was telling a fib. He was already very attracted to Molly. He narrowed his eyes, gazing at the bird. "How did you know? I didn't even say her name yet."

"Say her name," Jackson Jr mimicked him. "Say her name. Say her name." He continued to repeat the phrase until Eddie laughed and put both hands up.

"All right, all right. Her name is Molly. Molly Hessinger. She's just a woman I work with, Jackson Jr. so don't be getting any ideas."

"Molly. Molly, Molly, Little Dolly."

Eddie shook his head, amazed at the brain power of his pet friend. He went around the bar and into the kitchen, which was surprisingly large. He'd chosen the house because the rooms were large. Since the house was an average size, that meant there were fewer walls and rooms altogether. But he didn't care. He lived alone.

At first, it had been a strange feeling. He went straight from the farm life at his foster home to his own home right here in Vinton. From the age of sixteen until nineteen, he'd worked at a processing plant making tint for car windows. Andrew Lawler, his foster father's brother, hired him, knowing he was younger than he should have been working in the plant. At first, he'd been given easy jobs until he showed he was responsible and wouldn't get hurt. Then he moved to the higher paying positions, and at nineteen, ended up in the office at the plant, working on their media presence.

The job paid well and Eddie saved eighty percent of what he made for those four years of work. It had put the down payment on the house and bought him the Toyota, which was his pride and joy—after Jackson Jr., of course.

"Molly, Molly, Little Dolly," Jackson continued to utter the phrase. After about fifty times, Eddie usually told him to hush. He was an obedient bird and always did as he was told. But Eddie had never been teased about a woman before. He was surprised Jackson caught on to the emotion at all since he'd never seen Eddie in love with a woman before.

His thoughts caught him by surprise. Did he just think to himself that he was in love with Molly?

He had to laugh out loud. He wasn't in love with Molly. He pictured her in his mind and though his heart did warm over and he felt a happiness that was new to him; he didn't believe it was falling in love that was causing it.

Eddie had already gone through almost half his life without a woman, with very few people he considered friends—if any—and being alone was not new to him.

"She kind of looks like a doll," he eventually said, leaning back against the counter, a water bottle in one hand. He raised it to his lips and took a sip, sliding his eyes to his bird. "Molly Dolly. I wonder how she'd feel if I went into work and called her that." He chuckled to himself. He had no idea how she would react. He pictured her in his mind. She'd been so pleasant all day, he really didn't know what she looked like angry. He could picture her reacting with shyness, though.

Picturing that made Eddie's heart thump hard in his chest. She was too pretty for him to be picturing her like that. It might change the way he acted at work. That would be awkward, since he'd only been there one day. He didn't want anyone to taint this excellent job. He'd been wanting to work at the Inn for a very long time, mostly because it was surrounded by a beautiful length of woods in almost all directions except the actual shore where the water started. Even still, there was a bay where the Inn stood so that people could swim and would be protected, so to speak, from the larger body of water.

It was a beautiful place and the woods around it were filled with interesting creatures and plants of all kinds. He was going to explore those grounds the first opportunity he got.

His phone buzzed in his pocket and he whipped it out, hoping it was Molly, but not expecting it to be.

It was.

Hey, can you meet me at the Mantis restaurant on the eastern side of the Inn? I thought we could discuss some of your ideas you mentioned today. Around eight? Would that be alright with you?

Eddie stared at the text for a moment. Was she asking him out? Was it a business meeting only? How was he supposed to dress for this meeting? Would Steven be there?

His mind was flooded with questions as emotions stirred in his chest. He was nervous about a woman for the first time in his life. It was a feeling only associated when someone actually cared about something. And he cared about the impression he was making on her more than he wanted to admit.

"Okay," he said aloud, still staring at the text. "Give me a minute."

He looked up at Jackson Jr.

"Should I say yes or bow out for the night?" he asked, knowing the bird would repeat the last thing he said, as usual.

"Say yes," Jackson Jr. squawked. "Say yes. Say yes."

Eddie stared at the bird in astonishment.

He looked down at his cell phone and tapped out his response. He was going.

Chapter Four

Molly had thought she was nervous when she sent the text to Eddie asking him to meet her. But when she was seated at the restaurant and he wasn't there yet, she really knew what being nervous was all about. She tapped on the table with her fingers, scanned the other patrons in the restaurant, jiggled one leg up and down and hummed a little tune.

Alexander came over with a smile. "Good evening, Miss Molly. What can I get you to drink this evening?"

"I'll have a club soda, please."

"Certainly, coming right up."

He didn't leave right away and when she noticed, she gave him a direct look.

"Are you all right?" he asked softly, reaching out to touch his fingers to her shoulder.

She pulled in a deep breath and nodded. "Yes. I'm... meeting a new employee here and I'm very nervous about it."

"You want a drink?" Alexander's voice was suddenly serious. She knew he was teasing her, but only a little. He tilted his head down, keeping his eyes on her. "A real drink, I mean."

She laughed. "No, I gave up alcohol completely a few years ago, you know that. I don't want to be drunk around him either. God forbid!"

She didn't even want to think of such a thing. She shuddered visibly, making Alexander turn his head away to hide his smile, which he did rather unsuccessfully. It was okay, though. She knew Alexander was a friendly guy. He meant no harm.

"Well, best of luck to you with your new employee."

"Oh, he's not my employee," Molly hurried to say. Her words stopped Alexander, who had already spun away from her. He twisted his upper body so she knew he'd heard her. "He's a new employee here. At the Inn."

Alexander's thick brown eyebrows lifted and his equally dark brown eyes flashed mischievously. "Is that so? So... is it..." He left the words hanging, pushing out his lips and making a funny face at her. She knew what he meant.

She blushed. "I only met him today."

Alexander reacted with shock. "Today? And you already have a date with him? That's fantastic. You are quite the woman. I never would have expected that from you."

He winked again and sauntered off to get her soda water.

Molly felt her blush deepening. Her face was hot. She grabbed the water glass he'd brought to the table and gulped down a couple of swallows. The refreshing water cooled her off, but she waved one hand toward herself at the same time. The last thing she wanted was for Eddie to show up while she was looking flushed. Lord only knew what he would think of her.

"Come on, Moll," she muttered to herself. "Get it together."

When he did show up five minutes later, Molly was feeling better and had cooled down. Alexander would behave himself when he returned, she was sure. He wouldn't embarrass her. He wasn't the kind of friend that would do something like that.

Eddie smiled as he crossed the restaurant and slid into the booth seat across from her.

"This is a cute little restaurant. I've never been in here before. What's it, some kind of bistro or something? A café?"

Molly hadn't thought about it before, but as she scanned the room, she had to agree with him. The colors were bright and cheery, a pure bright white with very dark blue trim, mini-chandeliers over every table that glistened and running LED lights in all the trees and foliage placed around the place. It helped that there were arched windows running all around the place, giving it even more of a café feel.

"Yes, I suppose it is. It's very nice. They have some good cocktails here and brews from all around the world. I was particularly fond of Irish beer when I was drinking."

Eddie nodded, his eyes still roaming around them. When he spoke, it was in an absent-minded way. "I haven't had a drink in a decade. Probably won't drink again." His eyes finally settled on her face, making her heart thump hard. She swallowed, hoping he wouldn't notice her reaction. "I like the look of the place. Nice atmosphere and whatever they've got cooking back there, it smells delish."

Molly grinned. "I hope you're hungry. They have the best of everything in this place. You name it, you can get it."

Eddie lifted one eyebrow. "So not like a café, then. Even Mexican. Can I get some fajitas? An enchilada? Some plain tortillas just warmed over with a little butter on top?"

Molly let out a light laugh. "I... You know, I don't know. But the menu is right there." She gestured to the laminated pages glued together to her right. "Or you can download the menu if you have a bar scanner on your phone." She flicked the fingers of her left hand at the bar code laminated onto the table edge.

"I'll just do it the old-fashioned way, I think," Eddie replied, grabbing for the laminated menu.

He flipped it open. Molly tried to subtly watch him scanning the menu by flicking her eyes up and down. She didn't need the menu. She always got the same thing. Ham, turkey, and bologna on sourdough bread with mayonnaise and lettuce. Iced tea. French fries on the side.

"I think I know what I want," he said. "Do they make good club sandwiches here?"

Molly nodded. "I love their sandwiches. They make mine to my specifications and it's a lot like a club with turkey, ham, and bologna. I get mine on sourdough. You can get white, wheat, sourdough or rye here. Some of their sandwiches come on croissants, but you can't ask for them because they don't stock many back there. They'll only use them for the sandwiches they are supposed to be used for."

Molly thoroughly enjoyed the way he gazed at her the entire time she spoke.

"That's good to know, thank you," he said when she paused for a breath.

"You're welcome."

Her phone pinged a short note that let her know someone was contacting her text messenger. She blushed a little.

"I just need to make sure it isn't an emergency," she said softly as she rustled through her purse that was hanging off one side of her chair. She came up with the phone and glanced at the screen as she spoke. "My mother is ill at the moment and I like to make—"

She stopped speaking abruptly, staring at the message displayed on the screen.

Her heart thumped hard, but this time it wasn't because she was looking at an attractive man. This time, it was because she was frightened.

Molly pulled in a deep breath. She didn't want to suddenly end the dinner with Eddie so she could go find Steven. What if Eddie got the impression she wasn't interested after all and her chance with him was blown?

"Hey," Eddie said, getting her attention. She saw concern in his hazel eyes. "Are you all right? What's wrong? Is everyone okay?"

Molly had to make a quick decision.

Chapter Five

"I've received a strange text," she said quietly, turning her eyes to the left and right, scanning the other people in the restaurant. No one was looking at them. She hesitated another moment before laying the phone on the table, spinning it around 180 degrees and sliding it toward him.

He caught it before it could slide off and Molly watched as he read the words on the screen.

Of course, there would be no way for him to understand it. He knew far less about the situation that even she did. And she'd been working at the Inn for five years, friends with Steven for even longer.

"I don't understand," he said, sliding the phone back toward her. She appreciated the subtle nature with which he did the gesture and the fact that he was keeping his voice low. His face was serious but not too serious, and his eyes stayed directly on hers. "You are being blackmailed? What does this person want from you?"

Molly grimaced but smiled at the same time. She had no idea what kind of picture she made doing that but he didn't seem put off by it. He leaned in closer, saying quietly, "You can confide in me, Molly. I would never tell anyone your problems. Mostly because no one else probably cares. But also because that's not the kind of man I am. I care and I want to help."

Molly lifted her eyebrows, leaving her gaze locked with his. "Thank you for that, Eddie. And you're right. I can't imagine you telling anyone and it making much of a difference. Unless you're actually here to commit industrial espionage. You aren't the secret owner of a resort somewhere come to steal our secrets to success, are you?"

Eddie's lips pulled back in an impressively charming smile. "If I was," he said in a smooth voice, "I know exactly what I'd do. I'd just kidnap you... or get you to tell me all the secrets after befriending you and taking you out for coffee... I mean, no, I wouldn't do that..." He chuckled, lifting his eyes and scanning the ceiling as if it was the Sistine Chapel.

Molly laughed, despite the feeling of dread that had filled her to her very core. "Thank you for making me feel better," she said, "but I must tell you what this is all about. I guess with you working in the media department, you might want to be on the lookout for... for something to happen."

Eddie pulled his eyebrows together in confusion. "What are you talking about, Molly? What's going on? What did I walk into?"

Molly shook her head, hoping she could make clear what was happening at the Inn. "It's nothing life threatening," she said. "We've had some sabotage going on and some threatening letters, but Steven won't let us give in—not that we want to—so things just keep happening. Steven thinks he knows what's going on, but he has no proof."

"Well, what does he think is going on?"

Alexander returned at that moment, smiling at both of them. There was no sign on his face of the conversation they'd had before Eddie showed up.

"What can I get you to drink, sir?" the waiter asked. "And if you're ready to order, I can take that right now, as well."

Molly listened as Eddie ordered his club sandwich, adding French fries and telling them to make sure he had a dill pickle spear with his club sandwich. Alexander nodded vigorously.

"I'll make sure, no problem. Molly, you getting the same thing as usual?"

Molly smiled at him. "Yes, thank you." She was surprised by how easily the smile came to her, considering what had just happened. Her job, the Inn, it was all in jeopardy. All because someone was holding some kind of grudge.

"I think it's safe to say the Inn isn't going to shut down anytime soon," Eddie remarked after Alexander left. She gazed at his face, mesmerized by the serious look in his eyes. She didn't have to look at the text message to know he was referring to it.

It said her and Steven and the other members of her "gang," which only included Jack at the boatyard and Paula in the main restaurant kitchen, were to leave immediately or face the consequences.

"Why do they want you to leave?"

Molly shrugged, shaking her head. "I don't know. If Steven has a message from him telling him why, he hasn't shared it with us."

Eddie lifted his eyebrows. "Is that likely to be something he'd share with you?"

Molly nodded. "We've been friends for many years. He inherited the Inn, but he brought the rest of us along with him because it was in need of restoration, and he wanted to make it a success again. There was a little sabotage back then, but we figured out who that was."

"You're sure this isn't the same person?" Eddie asked, making it almost sound like a statement instead of a question.

Molly shook her head slightly. "No, that person is still in jail. And that was five years ago. This only started happening a month or two ago. I think Steven was the first one to get one of these. Now I'll have to change my number. Steven has had to change his several times."

Eddie looked irritated. "That must be a pain. Has anyone else received these messages? Or just you and Steven?"

"Paula and Jack get them, too. The kitchen pantry was set on fire and one of the boats was damaged. He's gone personal with Steven, though, flattening his tires and stuff like that."

"Have you reported it to the police?"

Molly sighed, thinking back on the conversations she'd had over the past several months with Steven and with the others, separately and together. "There isn't anything to take to the police. The first time it happened to Steven, and he did report it. They told him the number traced back to a burner phone. So, no luck there. We've each tried to report it at least once, but it's always a new burner phone they find in some trash can somewhere."

"I saw the security cameras. Has nothing been caught on them?"

Molly shook her head. "Nothing to show anyone doing anything bad. Like the vandalism of Steven's ride. Somehow the vandal found a way to avoid being seen as anything more than a blob or a shadow with no defining features."

Eddie looked thoughtful. Molly was anxious to hear what he had to say, so she kept quiet and leaned in toward him.

"You know," he finally said, "I might have the software to clean up those blobs and shadows. Pull out some of the defining features you're talking about. That would at least give us a face. Eventually, that will lead to a name, don't you think?"

"Well, fancy seeing you here!"

Molly's head snapped to the side as shock slid through her, making her feel ice cold inside. It was Steven, and she quickly warmed up.

"Oh, Steven, you gave me a start."

"Sorry about that," Steven replied apologetically, pulling a chair from a nearby table and placing it between his legs so he was facing the booth with his arms up on the back of the chair. "What are you two talking about?"

Molly grabbed her phone from the table and showed it to him. The pleasant look on his face was immediately replaced with one of irritation.

"This guy again," he murmured. "Ignore him."

"I can't," Molly replied bluntly. She saw the look of surprise on Eddie's face, but Steven just looked like he was listening. "Every time someone gets a text, some kind of sabotage happens within the next week or so. I don't even know what to look for."

Steven's voice was comforting when he leaned his head toward her and said in a quiet voice, "You will know something is off when you see it, Moll. You know you will. We can handle any storm, right? We aren't leaving the Inn, so we'll just have to put our heads together and work as one until we find out who this guy really is. Stay calm, okay? Just keep an eye out and be extra vigilant."

"All right," Molly agreed, hoping she could do exactly as he said.

Chapter Six

The strange incident and the mystery Eddie had stumbled into stayed on his mind the rest of that evening and through the night. He woke up the next day and it was the first thing that came to his mind.

His morning consisted of going into town to look at suppliers for the equipment he would need for his department. Steven had given him a blank check for furniture and decorations for his office. He wasn't the kind of person to take advantage of the generosity, so he was checking the local places and wanted to buy from a local shop, rather than a big corporation.

He showered, shaved, got dressed, and ate breakfast in the nook by the double glass doors that led out to his small veranda. He was fine with the porch area being fairly small. It was open to the most majestic landscape he could possibly have asked for. There were mountains in the distance cutting lines into the sky to the left and the right, coming together in a valley with a wide stream at the bottom winding toward his house and then jutting off to the left.

Many, many mornings he'd sat there watching the sunset. The sunrise was behind him and when it rose high enough to cast light over the top of his house, it shone directly onto the rippling water of the stream, creating almost a fireworks-type effect.

He was out the door by seven, ready to tackle the day with his usual enthusiasm. Which was not very much.

He slid into his Toyota and thought as he started the car that it actually was different that morning. This change he'd made in his life was already proving to be the start of a new chapter. Maybe this time in his life would prove to be more eventful than the last.

Eddie often pondered his mundane existence, praying for something to happen to him... anything... that would stand out in his memory and be something he could latch on to during depressive episodes. He didn't feel depressed often, but sometimes boredom drove him to it.

Eddie had never won an award. The only time he'd been on stage was to get his high school diploma. He'd never played a musical instrument. He didn't join in with the science club and didn't play sports. He was just Eddie Button, wizard on the computer. And he'd never won any awards for that, either.

It wouldn't have been so bad if he'd had an interest in building video games. He would probably be a billionaire by now with his knowledge, if only he'd had any kind of creative motivation whatsoever.

But he didn't. He just liked putting them together. And now that computers were a dime a dozen, his passion for building them was useless. It took him a lot more money to build one than the average person would spend going to a department store and buying one off the shelf.

So he'd formed an interest in media marketing and that's what he'd been doing for way too long now. He was almost forty years old. When was something going to happen?

A little twitch of energy in his chest made him feel excited. Maybe something *was* about to change in his life.

Eddie drove into Vinton, his thoughts more on the positive side than usual, which was nice. His eyes settled on a "NOW SERVING BREAKFAST" sign hanging overtop a brightly colored corner café he'd only been to once or twice.

He lifted his eyebrows, deciding to stop in and see what they had to offer for breakfast.

He recognized the lady behind the counter immediately and walked up to her.

"Emily?" He hoped he got the right name.

She looked up from the display case where she was adjusting pies on plates. Her eyes lit up when she saw him.

"Hey there! I'm sorry..." Her dark eyebrows pulled together. "I don't remember your name. So many people come through here."

"Eddie. Button. It's okay. Most people don't remember my name."

Emily's eyebrows shot up. "With a name like that, I'm surprised they don't. It suits you. How have you been? I can't remember the last time I saw you in here."

"I was passing and saw you're serving breakfast now. I haven't been in here for a while now. Just been holed up in my house, working, you know. I guess I'm not doing too bad. Especially now. How about you?"

Emily grinned, leaning on the counter with both arms stretched toward him. "You're just going to leave it like that, huh?" She laughed. Eddie realized why he remembered her. She was one of the few people he considered a friend in the city of Vinton. He'd made her laugh the last two or three times he was here and it was such a nice sound, it had given her a permanent place in his memory.

That was saying a lot, since Eddie's brain was filled with as much information as he could put in it, so only the important things held a permanent place there.

Emily's laugh was one of them.

"I'm doing okay," she responded. "Nothing much has changed except I finally got the morning shift I've always wanted. Now that we serve breakfast, I'm right where I want to be. I love getting off work in the early afternoon and having the rest of the day to do whatever I want. It's the perfect shift for me."

Eddie nodded. "I'm the same. Getting up early has always been easy for me. I wake with the sun, I guess."

Emily gave him a nod in return. "Why don't you sit up here at the bar? I can get you a cup of coffee or something."

"I'll take a cappuccino if you have them. A menu would be best. That way I can see what new breakfast foods you're offering."

He slid onto one of the stools at the bar as she slid a laminated one page front and back menu to him. She leaned in close, whispering loudly, "New cook behind the stove, too. Brady stayed on the night shift, thank goodness. He cooks eggs like he cooks his steaks. He doesn't have a clue how to handle them."

Eddie blinked at the woman. "I like his steaks," he said gently.

Emily chuckled. "I mean, he doesn't know how to handle eggs. He cooks eggs like he does steaks, raw, medium and well done."

They both laughed at that.

"You don't want him cooking your eggs for you. But this new guy back there, he's got the breakfast thing down. You're gonna love it, I promise."

"No matter what I get?"

Emily gazed at him directly. "Fact," she said simply.

Eddie was comfortable with that. He ran his eyes down the menu and was impressed with the low prices. He ordered something light because he'd already eaten at home, but he wanted to give the new cook a try.

"So, what is it you're so happy about, then?" Emily asked, returning from putting in his order. He gave her a questioning look. She rolled her eyes. "When you came in, hon. You said *especially now* and I want to know why things are going good for you right now. You must have something exciting to tell me."

"Ah! Yes." He grinned. "I've started a new job as the head of media at Oceanside Inn. You know the place out there..."

Emily's laugh made him let his words trail off. She waved one hand at him. "Honey, we all know about Oceanside Inn. That's great that you're working out there. God knows we all loved that old geezer that was there before. What was his name...?"

"Ben. Ben Smith."

"Yeah. Ben was a nice guy. Everybody liked him. I haven't heard any complaints about the new owner either..."

"Steven." A new voice joined theirs and they both looked at the tall man who had taken a seat next to Eddie. He smiled at them both. "Didn't mean to interrupt. Heard you mention Oceanside Inn."

Eddie glanced at Emily to study her face quickly. He didn't recognize the man who'd sat down. It was clear by the look on her face that Emily didn't know who he was, either.

Chapter Seven

Molly sat in the darkened room, her eyes staring at the monitor in front of her. She was glad the footage wasn't as grainy as some CCTV camera stuff she'd seen. It had never made sense to her until she'd worked with the system. Weather had a real effect on the quality and viability of anything the cameras produced.

She was watching the last month of footage from the boatyard. There were three cameras down there, one on the inside of the building from the back of the small "store" to the front counter, where transactions were made. Two were placed outside, facing the building from opposite sides.

She'd already been through Video A, which was one camera facing toward the building. She was now on Video B, which was the other side of the building. If she didn't see anything, she would try Video C, from inside the building, but didn't know what she could possibly see on that except people coming and going and making transactions. It wasn't like someone had robbed Jack or any of his employees that worked in the small dock shop. If she didn't see anything suspicious going on outside, how would she know who to look for inside? She couldn't just pick someone out because they looked suspicious to *her*.

She scooted back in the chair, her fingers splayed over her mouth and her thumb under her chin. Her elbow was on the armrest. She was bored.

Molly's eyes searched the screen. She blew a bubble with the gum in her mouth and popped it. She continued to watch the footage.

Sighing heavily, she leaned forward and pushed the fast-forward button. She kept her eyes glued to the screen as it flew past her. Thirty days was a long time to get through. The first tape had gotten more of her attention and produced exactly nothing. She didn't want to waste her time on this one that way. Something would pop up if there was anything to be seen.

A blip on the screen made her abruptly narrow her eyes.

"Whoa," she said softly, hitting the stop button and rewinding quickly to ten seconds previous. It wasn't far back enough, so she went twenty seconds back and stared at the video.

A black figure moved to the far right of the screen. The only reason she saw it was because she was looking. If a regular security guard had been watching, they wouldn't have seen anything.

Molly looked down at the keyboard, trying to remember what she needed to do to zoom in on a video. Photos were easy. Videos weren't.

Molly worked with the equipment to bring the footage closer, but as she did so, the image was lost in pixilation. Frustrated, she zoomed out until she thought it was the best visual representation of the man in the black hood and grey sweatpants she could get. She took a screen shot, and then took another with her phone.

There was a small notepad near her, which she pulled closer. She'd pushed a pen over her ear, so she retrieved it to jot down the date and time on the video footage.

She pushed the button to release that video and started up the one from inside the building. She ran the video forward until the time and date she'd jotted down.

Molly started about a half hour before the timestamp for the other video, when the man had appeared on the screen and then disappeared behind the trees beyond the boat dock. He was facing the building, so Molly had to assume he may have gone there.

She watched for the black hoodie and grey sweatpants combo for the entire day when he would have been on the property, as seen on Video B. He didn't go in the little shop.

Molly tapped the tip of her pen on the table, wondering where to go from there. She'd done what she was asked to do. Did Steven want her to continue looking through the footage? Maybe this guy was just a random visitor acting strangely.

Deciding she might see him again so she better keep watching, Molly switched back to Video B and let it play on 2f, which didn't move too quickly for her to spot something. She was reinvigorated now that she had something suspicious to look for. Or someone.

Her eyes were steady on the screen for so long it was starting to put a strain on her. She leaned forward and paused it at the same time as the door opened behind her. Molly swiveled in her chair to see Steven had entered.

"What's up?" he asked casually, closing the door and moving to the monitor table where she was. He looked up and scanned the cameras that were currently running. Seeing nothing suspicious there, he returned his eyes to her.

"I think I found something," Molly stated firmly. "I was going to call you when I reached the end of this footage. There's a man on here at..." She leaned forward. "Eleven in the morning on the fourteenth. I don't know what he was doing, but it looked to me like he was doing something suspish."

Steven pulled over a chair and sat in it, leaning forward. His long arms reached across the table in front of her and he maneuvered the tape to the time she mentioned. He stared at the footage of the man popping up and disappearing, playing it several times.

"And you enhanced the video as much as you could, right?" Steven asked.

Molly nodded. "Yeah, and took a picture at the closest clear distance I could get. Pull it in too far and you can't see anything but pixels."

Steven nodded. "I get it," he mumbled. "So this is the guy, huh? I think I agree with you. Especially because I'm pretty sure that's the same day the boat was sabotaged." Steven's face went taut when he mentioned the sabotage. Molly knew how much it bothered Steven. For five years, since he'd inherited the Inn, strange things had happened. People used the Inn to exact revenge on others or as a place to attempt to take their own lives. On his first day there, Steven had saved the woman he'd end up marrying from drowning.

It wasn't that the Inn was bad luck. It just seemed a central point for bad things to happen.

Molly wondered if there was a difference. That wasn't what Steven's Uncle Ben had intended for the place. She knew that, at least. He'd been a God-fearing man and did his best to provide excellent accommodations and service to the guests at the Inn. Molly remembered her visits there before she'd come to work for Steven. She and her friends always had a good time.

"Do you think Eddie might know how to make the video clearer when it's close up?" Molly asked, a tingle of nervous anxiety spreading through her when she mentioned him.

"Speaking of Eddie," Steven said in a voice that made Molly cringe slightly, but in a humorous way. "I thought I saw some sparks flying in my office yesterday. Did I? Hmm? Did I?"

Molly laughed softly, shaking her head. "I don't know, Steven. Eddie is... he's..."

"Perfect for you, is what he is," Steven stated boldly. "I just know it. Knew it the first time I saw him."

"Oh, you did not." Molly couldn't help laughing. "You didn't know that we would end up liking each other. Besides, if anything happens between us it won't be for a while."

Steven kissed the back of his teeth with his tongue. "That's ridiculous. You go for it. You're the only one in the gang who isn't married, and we need you to get married so you'll be like the rest of us. Group think, you know. We can't have any stragglers. It's time for you to get married."

Steven made it through his little speech without laughing, but Molly didn't. She pictured being booted from the Inn because she wasn't married at the age of thirty-eight and it only made her laugh harder.

"We'll have to see what happens, Steven. I promise you'll be the first to know."

Chapter Eight

"Do you know Steven?" Emily asked. Eddie detected a hint of suspicion in her voice. He returned his gaze to the new customer, wondering what she saw in the man that made her react that way. Or maybe that was the way women reacted when a strange man sat down and injected himself into her conversation with someone else.

"I know of Oceanside Inn," the man replied smoothly, seeming not to have heard the same suspicion Eddie heard. "I've been there a few times as a guest. It's nice. Lots of unexplored land there."

Eddie thought that was probably the strangest thing he'd heard in a long time. It sparked his interest, though, because he'd had a similar thought when he first saw the property.

"What do you mean by that?" Emily persisted. Eddie flicked his eyes between them during their conversation.

The man raised his eyebrows at her. He held out one thin hand. "Vincent LaBrock," he introduced himself. "Yeah, that's my real name. People call me Vinnie. I'm not in the mafia, don't worry. There are no Sopranos in my family line and I don't know a thing about waste management."

Eddie laughed. He saw the man was successfully working his way into Emily's affections. Her small smile reflected that. She was trying not to like the guy, he could tell. But despite the air of suspicion that hung around him, he was showing himself to be pretty charming.

"So..." Emily continued, "what did you mean by unexplored land? I think Steven has done a good job

45

refurbishing and renovating that place since his uncle died and there was that fire and all that other stuff that happened."

Eddie pulled back a little, staring at the woman. She caught his look and turned her eyes to him. "Surely you know about all that stuff happening. I'd think that would be common knowledge if you live here in Vinton."

Eddie nodded. "I guess I just didn't expect for *everyone* in Vinton to know about it all. It wasn't in the paper for very long. Wasn't front page news."

Emily's eyes went soft, and she tilted her head to the side. "You think I speak for everyone in Vinton? How sweet."

They laughed together.

"I'll tell you what I meant," Vinnie said when their laughter died down. "I just meant that... the land itself has been left unexplored. I think Steven could be doing a lot more than he is to preserve the natural habitat of the place. I mean, there's got to be conservationists out there who know of ways to prevent further construction to the place." He gave Eddie a direct look. "You said you were just hired as the head of a new department, is that right? Steven is adding a new department to the Inn?"

Eddie was suddenly flooded with fresh suspicion. He tried not to react to the emotion but the man's direct questioning and the way he asked them reminded Eddie of reporters but ones he'd seen on TV. He'd never been in a situation where he was surrounded by reporters asking questions, so he didn't know if it was like that in real life. Vinnie definitely reminded him of TV reporters.

"Yes," he replied, losing his grin and narrowing his eyes instinctively. "The media department."

Vinnie seemed oblivious to what Eddie felt had to be obvious signs that he was not laughing about or enjoying the sudden line of conversation.

He turned his head away and looked down at the coffee cup he'd brought to the bar with him. Eddie realized Vinnie must have been sitting at a booth behind him, listening to his conversation with Emily.

"Where are your offices going to be?" Vinnie asked pointedly, turning his entire upper body this time. He placed one hand on his thigh and continued without waiting for the answer. "I know the layout of that property. I did a sketch of it while I was visiting one time. I walked the entire perimeter to see how long it would take. Made notes of all the twists and turns of that inlet and the streams that come off it. You know, around the docks, creeping up onto the land."

Eddie listened to the man, blinking silently. Vinnie's long face showed passionate emotion as he spoke about the sketches and notations he'd made. By the end of his description, Eddie was sure the man knew where every rock was placed on Steven's land.

He didn't know what Steven would think about that, but if it was *his* land, Eddie would be uncomfortable with someone making detailed blueprints of the property. Even if they were only sketches. Why did he need to know the exact layout of the building? If he was sketching landscapes and beauty, Eddie would understand. But from the way he spoke of it, Vinnie was making literal blueprints of the property.

"Are you a surveyor?" The question came out before he could stop it. His question got a reaction from Emily, who slapped the counter in front of them and pointed at Vinnie.

"That's it!" she exclaimed. "You're a surveyor. What, you working for the Virginia government or something? I'm sure Steven isn't doing anything wrong. If he's building onto the Inn, I'm sure he's got all the right permits and all th—" She stopped speaking. Vinnie was shaking his head.

"I'm not a surveyor," Vinnie responded. "And I don't work for the Virginia government. I do this for me."

"But why do you need details about the property?" Eddie asked, feeling bolder with Emily on the other side of the counter, whom he was sure was on his side of things. She'd been the first one to be suspicious of Vinnie. It had taken him a minute or two, but he saw quickly through the charm.

As for Vinnie, he seemed completely unaware that the two of them were suspicious at all.

"It is a personal matter. I'm hoping Steven isn't planning to build onto the building. Too much change is... is traumatic for the earth, you know. The environment. It stirs up the... little creatures and critters in the area. Disturbs their natural habitat."

Eddie's suspicion of the man was now so strong, he was sure Vinnie would notice. His hesitant speech, his stumbling over words and apparent search for the right ones only made things worse for him. But Eddie was wrong. Vinnie didn't notice. He continued on.

"Plus, there's at least one wing left that's still closed off—"

"It's under construction now," Eddie injected, figuring if Vinnie could come over and highjack the entire conversation, why shouldn't he do the same thing? "Steven isn't planning on adding to the building, as far as I know. The only construction that's being done is on that last wing you're talking about. It will be made into more guest rooms. Not anything else. And I just have my one office. I'm the head of the department, but also the only employee in that department, at least for now."

"Ooo, does that mean you get to hire employees of your own?" Emily looked at him with excited eyes.

He grinned at her, relieved that she was there to lessen the tension he was feeling. "Why? Are you looking to change jobs?"

She tilted her head back and laughed. "I know absolutely nothing about that technical jargon you do in your head while you're sleeping, Eddie. I wish I did because I'd come and work for you."

"That's a really nice thing to say, Emily. Thanks for that this morning. And thanks for this coffee. I gotta get to the supply store. Lots of things to do this morning."

"You be safe and careful out there, Eddie. And come see me again soon."

Eddie was stunned when Emily reached over the counter with both hands and pulled him into what he called a "distance shoulder hug," when there was just enough contact to actually make it a hug but it was basically only the cheeks that connected at any point.

"Thanks, Emily. You, too."

"Talk again sometime!" Vinnie raised one long arm and smiled at Eddie.

Eddie left not knowing whether he'd just made a couple friends or just one.

Chapter Nine

"The boat *was* sabotaged on the same day," Steven said, pulling his cell phone from his ear. He didn't bother hitting the end button, so Molly assumed the other person had hung up. "Lisa said it was about an hour after that footage of the man we saw skulking around."

"I think we should go check out the area where that man was. We might find something useful to give the police."

Molly was unhappy with their local police force. Five years ago, when they'd had a fire caused by a customer who'd gone crazy, they'd had some help in the form of two capable detectives.

Not only were they gone from the police force now, their replacements were incompetent and uncaring. It was a man and a woman, so Molly knew it wasn't because of sex that they were ambivalent to the problems at the Inn. They shoved the case on a shelf, never to be looked at again. It was unimportant. Because of their attitudes, Steven had decided to take on the investigation himself, with the help of Jack, Molly, and Paula. His wife, Dani, offered to help but Steven was adamant that she stay away from anything dangerous, as she was carrying their unborn twins and he was as nervous as he could get.

"I think you're right," Steven replied, nodding. "Let's go now, unless you have something else you're doing."

Molly shook her head, standing up. "No. I reserved the whole day to look into this. I don't like that text I got yesterday. I don't know what to look for or anything so I thought the best thing to do was come here and look at the footage. If we can catch this guy before he attacks the financial department, I won't have to worry about you losing everything you own."

Steven held out his hand to the door, pushing it open with the other. She went through in front of him and he followed behind her. "I don't think he's going to attack my finances."

Molly turned her head to look up at him as they walked side by side down the hallway to the front doors. "What do you mean? I got the text. He has to be coming after me next."

Steven looked thoughtful, and Molly was anxious to hear what he was thinking. He was a problem solver, to say the least, and she was grateful to have his advice. "So far, everything he's done has been physical. He stole from Paula and wrecked some of the equipment in the kitchen of the main restaurant and he sabotaged a boat. He slashed some tires and broke some CCTV cameras. I haven't seen him do anything electronic except text and any five-year-old can do that. I'm surprised he isn't sending notes with the letters cut out of magazines."

Molly nodded at him. "I suppose you're right. But I don't want to get hurt. What if he cuts my brake lines or something? And why is he even going after me to begin with? Why any of us? Teresa had to leave because of this. I'm not going to leave. I can't. This is my home."

Steven didn't say anything. She knew how he felt about Teresa Knox leaving their employment so abruptly. The girl hadn't even let them know she wasn't coming in. She just stopped coming. Tanner asked if he should go searching for her, but Molly said no. She understood why Teresa had left. Why would she stay when she was receiving messages like that?

She'd consulted Steven, and he'd agreed with her. There was every chance things could get so much worse. Molly often thought about Dani and the unborn twins. The police might not take these text threats, Teresa's departure, and the sabotage seriously, but Molly and her friends didn't have a choice. It wasn't just money and employees the saboteur was costing. It was peace of mind.

They were heading down the white concrete sidewalk that led to the boat dock when Molly spotted Jack in the distance. He was talking to someone who looked familiar. A shot of adrenaline went through her when she realized it was Eddie.

What was he doing talking to Jack? What could he possibly have to talk about? As far as she knew, he didn't know Jack at all.

"Look, there's Eddie," Steven said. "I never did answer your question about the video, did I?" He gave her a big, teasing grin and she knew exactly what he was talking about.

She pursed her lips and narrowed her eyes at him. "All right, let's not start that again. I told you... we'll see. Anyway, no, you didn't."

"Yesterday, before he left, I caught up with him and told him a little more about the situation. I asked if he would help out if we needed him for anything."

"Did you really." Molly didn't ask the question. It wasn't out of the realm of possibilities for Steven to immediately trust someone else. Besides, he was the one who hired Eddie. They had to have spoken on several occasions for him to put Eddie in charge of their media presence. That was a big thing now. It was great for advertisement but also opened up the Inn to trolls and people who just want to stir the pot.

She was glad she wasn't in control of it.

"I wonder what he's doing talking to Jack."

Steven's voice was low and serious. Molly glanced at him. They were about to find out the answer. Steven would ask without hesitation if he had to. But he didn't have to.

Jack and Eddie saw them. It was Jack who went into action immediately, turning to walk up the rest of the concrete sidewalk to meet them.

"Hey! Can't believe you guys came down here right when we were talking about you."

Molly raised her eyebrows and gave them a questioning look. She didn't say anything because she knew she didn't have to. Steven would sort things out, as always.

"Hope it was good things," he said. The words underlying his tone were obvious to Molly. She wondered if Jack and Eddie had heard it.

Jack did.

"Eddie's got experience with boats," he said simply. "Came down to offer any assistance I might need. Call-in or a no-show or something, you know."

Molly and Steven both nodded at the boatman.

"I've got something to tell you guys," Eddie said. "I didn't know Jack was another one of your, uh, gang?"

Molly laughed softly.

Steven nodded at the newcomer. "Yeah, in college me and Molly, Jack, Paula, and our friend Andy, who isn't here anymore, were dubbed the Musketeers so we just kind of stuck with each other. Long gap between seeing each other and now it's every day, isn't that right, Molly?" He grinned at her.

She smiled back. "That's right, Steven."

"I'm sorry to hear about your friend," Eddie said seriously.

Molly and the others stared at him. Steven raised his eyebrows and realization came to his face.

"Oh! You mean Andy. He's not dead or anything. He lives in North Carolina now in a big mansion that some might actually consider Heaven."

"Oh, Steven," Molly said with a laugh.

Eddie smiled and laughed in a breathy way. "Oh, well, that's good. Thank God for that."

"We did," Molly said, hoping he caught on to what she meant. "He's in a very happy, comfortable place in his life with his new wife. They are a lovely couple. She's the one whose family donated the money for the renovations two years ago."

"I like to hear that," Eddie offered with a nod. "So I really need to tell you about this guy I met at a café this morning. It was kind of creepy, if you ask me. He wasn't unfriendly or anything like that. But he started asking about the Inn because I told Emily behind the counter that I worked here. He was asking questions like a reporter—that's what I was thinking at the time." He moved his eyes to his three companions individually, settling on Molly's. He gestured slightly with his hands as he spoke.

"What kind of questions was he asking?" Steven's voice sounded hard.

Molly couldn't help letting her mind wander as she admired Eddie. She couldn't quite put her finger on it, but there was something about the man whom she'd assumed was somewhat standoffish and maybe a loner in real life. There was something about the way he was relating the story that made it impossible to question him. There was no doubt in her mind that what he was saying was the absolute truth. It was fascinating to watch.

Chapter Ten

Eddie could barely wait to tell them about Vinnie. He'd pulled into the parking lot and his eyes dropped down to the boat dock when he got out of the Toyota. He saw Jack and remembered Steven mentioning Jack knew all about what was going on.

He'd practically run down the slanted sidewalk to get to the man and was out of breath when he got there. Still, Jack listened with the patience of a saint, supplying words when Eddie didn't get them out.

Now, as he told the story to Molly and Steven, Jack stood back and let him talk. Eddie was so appreciative of Jack, he made a mental note to see if the man was free to get a beer sometime. He'd say beer because that's what he was expected to say. Eddie didn't have many men he called friends. He couldn't think of even one if he tried. It was about time he made a few new ones.

And not creepy, weird ones like Vinnie LaBrock.

"He came up and sat down right when I said I started working here. Emily got it out of him that he wasn't a reporter or TV personality. He was very energetic, like he thought he was stage or something. Or maybe on camera. I did look for cameras hidden somewhere, but I didn't see anything. I think that's the point of calling them hidden. They can't be seen by the naked eye."

He pondered that thought now that he'd said it out loud. He pictured Vinnie in his mind.

"We've got some video footage from a couple weeks ago," Molly said. "I think we should let you look at it. There's a strange man on there. We can't really see him, but well, he's just acting strange, that's all. Maybe it's the same guy."

Eddie was willing to bet it was Vinnie. He lifted his hands and said firmly, "He said he has blueprints or drawings of the property and everything on it. I believe him. He looks like the type to do something creepy like that. He said he's visited a few times and while he was staying here, he made the blueprints."

Steven frowned. "Why does he have drawings of my Inn?" he asked. "What did he say when you questioned him about that?"

Eddie shook his head. "He said he wants them. He was vague, didn't answer my question at all."

"You haven't told us his name," Jack said, prompting Eddie to say,

"Vinnie LaBrock."

He saw no strange reaction from his companions, so he didn't give the disclaimer Vinnie added to his.

"First, I want to go to the area where we saw him at," Molly said, her eyes moving to the distance on the other side of the inlet where the boats were docked. "Then we can look at the video footage again."

"Probably also want to check the log for dates when he stayed here," Steven mumbled. When he started walking toward the boat dock building, the others followed along. Eddie hurried to keep up with them as they strode confidently around the building on an outside path that would take them around to the other side. A long boat shed stretched out, half of it overtop water, half over the land. Just before they got to that building, Steven halted, his eyes turning to Molly.

"This is about where we saw him, right?"

Molly stopped and looked around her. She nodded. "Yeah. I think so."

Eddie dropped his eyes to the ground and examined the rocks, dirt, and grass. He took a few steps in either direction, his eyes on the ground. He saw nothing strange.

In truth, Eddie didn't know what he was looking for.

As soon as he thought the words, Molly murmured an answer. She appeared to be talking to herself, but Eddie heard her. He didn't acknowledge that he did, though. He wanted to hear what she was saying and not interrupt her.

"Okay, hmmm," she said in a quiet voice as she narrowed her eyes and studied her surroundings. "We gotta look for anything out of the ordinary that shouldn't be here. He might have been smoking. Maybe a cigarette butt while he waited? Or maybe he left a bomb hidden somewhere around here."

"Doubtful," Steven said quickly, his voice louder than hers. Eddie was glad he wasn't the only one listening to Molly talk to herself. Or maybe she was making suggestions to them. Either way, Eddie appreciated it. He stopped concentrating only on the ground and looked closely at the trees, too. There was only one with a hole in the side. He hesitated a moment before sticking his fingers in the hole. He closed his eyes and prayed there wasn't a critter in there that might bite his fingers off. His body went tense but relaxed when he felt only bark on the inside.

"You never know," Molly continued. "But I think you're right. It's doubtful. We saw him here two weeks ago, or ten days to be exact. I'd think his bomb would have gone off by now."

"Just be careful."

Eddie hated that they were going to be leaving empty handed, but he didn't see anything out of the ordinary and neither did the others. As they walked, disappointed, back to the sloping sidewalk up the hill, he tried to think of ways to comfort Molly. She didn't seem to need any comforting, but that didn't stop his desire to give it to her.

Jack stayed behind to resume his duties, but they swore they'd keep him in the loop.

"I'm going to check the logs while you and Eddie look at that footage," Steven stated. "I'll meet you in the VT room."

He strode off in the direction of the main building, his long legs making it seem shorter than it was. When Molly turned her head and looked at him, Eddie's heart did a leap in his chest. He smiled at her with a closed mouth.

"I guess it's just the two of us. I think you'll be able to see if it's the same guy from the footage, probably based on, like, size and height and all of that."

Eddie nodded. "I guess we'll see."

"It was two weeks ago," Molly replied with a grin, "but I don't suppose he was wearing a black hoodie with grey sweatpants, was he?"

Eddie chuckled as he responded. "No, sorry. He was dressed regular, jeans and a t-shirt with a jacket. No sweat suit of any kind."

"Dark hair?"

Eddie let out his laugh this time. "Let me look at the tape, Miss Anxious. We'll know in a few minutes, anyway. And yes, he had dark hair."

Molly laughed with him. "Thank you for that. It's just... nice to maybe put a name to the face and the... well, the feeling, too. These texts..." Her face seemed to collapse upon itself. Eddie was filled with the desire to grab hold of her and hold her. "They... they really make me scared, Eddie. I know the others are pretty dismissive of them, but... well, what does he want?"

Eddie held back from what he wanted to do, choosing to talk about Steven instead.

"Someone has a grudge against Steven. If it's Vinnie, by the way he talked, I swear it was like he wanted control of the place. He talked about Steven making renovations and saying he shouldn't be building any additions on or anything like that."

Molly frowned. "What are you... I mean, what is he talking about? There are no additions to the original building. It's big enough. We're just now doing that last wing where the roof collapsed during the heavy snow last year. That's not adding on."

"I know. I pointed that out."

"Well, how did Mr. LaBrock take that?"

"He talked about the valley cutting through the two mountains and how pretty it is during the sunset because the sun likes to go down in that spot."

"That has nothing to do with adding on to the house."

Eddie nodded. "I know. He answered like that every time I asked him what his business was with Steven. I thought it was strange enough he called him Steven. That seems really familiar. So maybe this will turn out to be someone Steven knows who is after him."

Molly turned serious eyes his way. "We need to tell Steven that when he gets here. He didn't seem to know the name, but... well, we don't even know if it's real, do we?"

Chapter Eleven

Molly cued up the video and let it play for Eddie. She held her phone up and made a video of it to show to others without having to bring them into the VT room.

He sat in front of the screen and played the video over and over. She watched his face, hoping to see some kind of recognition, but all she saw was doubt.

Finally, he pushed away from the monitor a little and shook his head at her. "I can't tell. It could be him, yes. The height looks just about right, I think. But I can't be certain. I wouldn't swear that was him if I was in court."

Molly sighed. That was what she'd expected. She shook her head, putting one hand on his arm to comfort him. "It's all right," she said. "I didn't expect you to recognize him. He's just too far away from the camera. It's not made for seeing hundreds of yards away, right?"

"Right." He still looked disappointed, and she didn't blame him. She was hoping even though she knew the chances were slim.

Steven appeared a few minutes later, slipping through the door so quietly Molly wouldn't have known he was there if she hadn't seen him herself.

"He registered here twice," Steven said immediately, holding out a photocopy of the logbook at the front desk. It was a tradition at Oceanside Inn for the guests to sign into the huge leather-bound logbook when they stayed there. No one had ever minded the practice.

"All right, I have a question," Eddie said, putting up one finger. "If he's signing in and staying as a guest and going around making a map of the place, wouldn't that signify he's casing the place? But if he is, why is he using his real name?"

"It might not be his real name. Maybe it's just the one he's using now."

Molly thought Steven had a good point. If it wasn't, that would make things more difficult. He could disappear at any time, free to sabotage someone else for no reason.

"Here's what I'm thinking," Steven said as he pulled a chair over and sat in it. He looked Molly directly in the eyes as he spoke, moving his gaze to Eddie every now and then to include him in the conversation. "What we've got so far and that's if, of course, it's Vinnie who's doing this in the first place. One, we don't have a motive because we don't know him. You have the best chance of fixing that, Eddie."

Molly's eyes slipped to Eddie to see he looked surprised. "I do?" he asked.

Steven nodded. "You have spoken with him on a friendly basis. I'm surprised that he talked to you, knowing you work here. That's one thing against him being the villain in our scenario."

"Okay, so we don't have a motive for Vinnie yet and you want me to talk to him and see what he's got up his sleeve?"

Eddie sounded fine with that, even if he had looked a bit scared before.

"Two, we've got a link to him being near the dock before the boat was sabotaged a couple weeks ago. He's on video camera skulking about. Unfortunately, I don't think that alone is near enough to convict him."

Molly shook her head. "No, of course not. It will take a lot more than that."

"And we have the dates of his visits coinciding with the sabotage on both occasions," Steven said in a hopeful tone. "Either way, the more evidence we gather, the more we'll have to present to the detectives." He said the last word with complete disdain, a look of disgust that was rare for Steven coming to his face.

"What do you want me to do?" Eddie asked. "Search him out in town? Are we going to wait for him to make another visit or—"

"We can't wait," Molly interrupted him, saying her words sharply. Her heartbeat raced as she thought about the text messages she'd received. "We have to find him before he does something to me."

Molly was a little surprised and a lot pleased to see a look of concern on Eddie's face. She even thought he made a slight move, as if to come to her and maybe give her a hug. She wished he would.

"You're right," Eddie said. "I'm sorry. I wasn't thinking. We need to act now. I'll go into town and search for him, if you want. I'll make a citizen's arrest and force him to tell me what evil machinations he's up to."

Molly gave Eddie a small grin, and the gesture made her feel better in an instant.

Steven was also amused by Eddie's suggestion. "If only," he replied. "Yeah, look for him and call or text me when you find him. Keep an eye on him and I'll be on my way as soon as you text. Sound good?"

Eddie blinked at Steven and asked a question that sent Molly into hysterical giggles. She had to turn away from the men and hide the giggles behind her hand.

"Shouldn't I be working?"

Steven let out a sharp laugh. "You *are* working. For me. As the boss, I'm requesting you do this." He lifted one hand and made a circle overtop all their heads. "Then, when this is finished, you can go back to your stuff."

"I... I have a bunch of people coming with supplies for my office. Furniture and stuff they are delivering, you know. I... shouldn't I be there for them?"

Steven shook his head. "No need. I'll get someone to wait for them and show them around. Feel free to move stuff around once you get back in there. I want you to be comfortable there. I predict in the next couple months, things will be rough with you. Then maybe life will be peaceful again."

"I do hope that happens."

Molly listened to their conversation devolve into friendship banter and cleared her throat loudly.

"Can we get back to solving this problem so I don't get killed, please?" she asked, pretending to pout.

Both men laughed. She was amused to see Eddie turned red as a beet.

"So you want me to go right now, then?"

Steven lifted his eyebrows. He glanced down at the cell phone screen in his hand. "I mean, it's almost eleven. How about we get an early lunch? We can do it down on the dock, since the weather is so beautiful. Maybe go for a little trip in the pontoon."

"Surely there isn't enough time for all that," Eddie said, sounding astounded.

"We can take as long as we want," Steven responded in a firm voice. "I own this joint."

Eddie and Steven talked as they left the VT room, with Molly following close behind him. She didn't mind that they seemed oblivious to the fact she was even there. They had made fast friends, and she liked that. She was enjoying watching Eddie's form walk, thinking how smooth he was.

Steven definitely didn't mind the fact that the man was so much shorter. He was almost a foot taller than the other man. It was noticeable enough that it didn't need to be mentioned.

It had been a long time since she and her friends had gathered on the pontoon. She thought about how different things were now from five years ago. Andy was gone and the rest of them had settled into their positions—Jack with his nurse wife who worked in the clinic on the hillside, and Steven with his Dani and their expected twins, Paula with her sous chef husband, Jimmy selling their recipes for a hundred dollars a pop. So much success in both personal and business.

Molly had the business thing down.

Now it was time to concentrate on the personal.

Chapter Twelve

The afternoon lunch invitation turned into a dinner invitation when Steven was called to the construction site of the renovation unexpectedly.

Eddie readied himself in front of the full-length mirror attached to the back of his door. He had never prepared himself to go out the way he was now. He even had some kind of gel in his hair. He'd applied it lightly, and the waves fell just right. He grinned, knowing it was lopsided, as always. The right side lifted up higher than the left. It had been like that all his life.

"Ready to go make an impression?" he asked his reflection before giving himself a thumbs up.

"Lookin' sharp," Jackson Jr. said from his perch in his cage, which was hanging by the window.

Turning away from the mirror, Eddie gave the bird a big smile. "Why thank you, my friend," he said, happily. He strode to the front door as Jackson Jr. repeated the phrase twice more and gave a low whistle, to which Eddie couldn't help chuckling. He reached to the side to take the keys from the table. His jacket hung on a hook beside the door.

His confidence wasn't as solid as his mirror might have gotten the impression. In fact, he was surprised he was even able to go to the dinner. On normal occasions, he bowed out of such events without even bothering to give it a second thought. Jackson Jr. was a great encouragement. But this was the first time he'd done this, really.

He knew the reason for his change of heart where social matters were concerned. Then again, that very reason—Molly—was why he was feeling so anxious at the moment. He didn't like the feeling, never had. Maybe that's why he'd blocked it out and denied any relationships could form with a woman.

Molly had made a difference without even trying. She'd brought him out of the shell he'd lived in for over a decade. Almost two, really. He'd bought the house so young. He'd lived there alone the entire time since.

And now the lifelong bachelor had met his match.

Eddie liked the analogy, especially because he felt like his attraction to her had been a nice smack to the face. It was suddenly there. No warning given. His heart came to life. He felt the air in his lungs and the blood in his veins. He blinked and saw the world before him and the possibilities it had to offer.

It was like seeing color for the first time.

He slid into the driver's seat of his Toyota and started the engine.

They weren't meeting at the restaurant of the Inn. Instead, Steven had suggested a nice restaurant that was just across from the café where he'd seen Vinnie LaBrock.

That was no coincidence, Eddie was sure, but Steven didn't say anything about Vinnie when he texted about it.

Anticipation made Eddie's skin tingle as he drove toward the heart of Vinton. The café—or the restaurant to which he was going—weren't really that far away. When he pulled into the parking lot, the first car he saw was Molly's.

The lot was quite full, and there were only one or two spots left. One of them happened to be next to Molly's car. He blinked in amazement and drove toward it. When he turned the Toyota into the spot, he saw a reserved sign on the pavement's edge in front of it.

It wasn't metal like the usual reserved signs. It was written on a piece of wood that was attached to a pole which was stuck in the ground.

Under the word RESERVED, it said the word EDDIE.

Eddie had never felt so privileged in his life. He was doubly surprised the other patrons in the restaurant even cared what the sign said. It looked handmade because it was.

He was inside searching for his new friends seconds later. He spotted them just as a waitress came over, a pleasant smile on her face.

"Welcome!" she said enthusiastically. "You are joining the Smith party?"

Eddie nodded. "Yes. Steven Smith."

The waitress stepped back, handing him a menu at the same time.

"Please take your menu. It will save us both extra trips. Let one of us know if you need anything at all. Okay?"

Eddie was taken aback by her sudden business tone.

"Okay, yes. Thank you so much."

"You are welcome. I'll be over shortly with some water and bread for you."

"Yes, thank you."

With that, she was off to take the orders of people who weren't late to their parties.

He watched the group as he approached, thinking how strange it felt to be suddenly surrounded by people who had literally known each other all their lives. Would they even accept him into their huge circle?

Not to mention all of them were married except Molly, and his interest in her was probably obvious. He didn't feel too bad about that since the feeling seemed to be mutual. He wasn't a man to turn away from potential adventure and fun. He could think of many museums and parks he wanted to take her to, tours they would enjoy together. He thought about it all the time. He kept his eye on the paper and noticed every time there was an event he would have liked to attend with her.

This, after a few days.

Eddie reached the table and sat next to Molly, the only open chair. He turned to his right and greeted Steven's wife, Dani, who, in Eddie's opinion, looked like she was going to explode.

"How are you?" he asked, dropping his eyes to her belly and then up to her eyes again.

"I'm doing well. Thank you for asking. They must have told you I fell in the convenience store."

"I'm sorry, no, but wow, that's terrible. Glad to see you're okay."

She smiled at him and turned away when someone said something to her. Eddie looked around at everyone, his eyes finally settling on Molly, who was pulling small bits off the fluffy biscuit she was holding and placing them in her mouth between words. She and Jack were having a conversation.

"I don't think I've met you yet." He heard a voice behind him and turned to see a tall woman with a man beside her, both smiling at him. He felt a twinge of anxiety in his chest and forced a smile.

"No, I don't think so," he replied.

"I'm Paula and this is my husband, Jimmy. We're the chefs in the Inn restaurant, you know."

He nodded, relief sweeping over him. Who had he expected? Of course it was Paula and her husband. Eddie scolded himself softly for being so anxious. It was natural, but he still didn't like it. He wanted to be confident. He wished he could be.

But Eddie wasn't the type of man who would dwell on problems like that. He was proud of himself when he did something good and berated himself when he did something wrong. He'd learned to live with himself a long, long time ago. The circumstances of his life had made him as independent as a person could be. He pulled himself out of each crisis that occurred and gave himself credit for doing so.

Molly's eyes flitted over to him. She smiled and warmed his heart.

"Are you having a good time?" she asked.

He shrugged, keeping his eyes on hers. He liked it when she looked directly at him. "I just got here. I hope I do. I'm sure I will. But I don't know yet."

Molly leaned toward him, her smile intact. "Well, I'll make sure you do. Besides, we're here kind of on a stakeout, aren't we? And you're the only one who really knows what he looks like. Sure, I'll go crazy if a see a pair of grey sweatpants and a black hoodie, but you... you got an actual look at his face. He talked to you."

Molly sounded excited about the prospect of nabbing Vinnie from the café. Eddie thought it was exceedingly cute. However, the chances of seeing Vinnie at the deli across the street were really very slim.

"You're right, of course," he said, deciding to give in to her. He was just glad to be included in the mystery solving. The sabotage had been going on long before he got there, so to be involved with his direct boss, the owner, and the other heads of management at the Inn was a great start to his new career.

Chapter Thirteen

The night was going smooth. Molly was glad she and her friends were able to put their worries aside long enough to have some laughs. Toward the end of the night, the conversation around the table became more serious and voices lowered.

It began with Paula asking Steven if he'd heard from Andy. He'd looked at Eddie for the first part of his answer and then his plate for the rest of it.

"Andy is the other member of our little group. I think you remember I told you about him."

Eddie nodded.

"He's doing all right," Steven continued. "His wife is the one who funded the reconstruction of a lot of the Inn. I had to get investors. There was so much going wrong. It costs a lot of money to redo the plumbing in a building as large as the Inn, especially with everything that's attached to it. The swimming pool and the tennis court. They may not be the biggest you can find anywhere, but they make this place a little more special."

Molly noticed Steven said "this place," even though they weren't at the Inn. That was a sure sign he'd been spending too much time there. He automatically assumed that's where he was twenty-four-seven.

"It's a resort to be proud of." Molly had to say something. "The guests love it. They leave good reviews online. I'm sure Eddie will incorporate some of them in the new media social online presence, or whatever it's called." She grinned at Eddie. "Maybe I'll be an influencer."

Eddie raised one eyebrow. "You scoff, but a woman of your talents, skills, and looks can make a lot of money."

Molly huffed at what he was saying, letting her eyes sweep across the rest of her friends, secretly wondering if any of them agreed with Eddie. They weren't saying it out loud, but Molly didn't miss the look on Steven's face. He knew what was going on. Oh, how he knew.

"I'm too old for that," she responded dismissively. "That's for twenty-year-olds."

"I don't think it's something you'd want to do, Molly," Eddie said, leaning over to her, forcing her to look deep into his hazel eyes. She tried to calm her heart as he continued, "I'm just saying it's something you *could* do if you wanted to, and you'd make money through advertisers. That's where the money is, you know. Unless you're doing the risqué stuff."

"Nope." Molly shut that down quick. She lifted one hand and made a chopping motion in the air. "That's not going to happen."

Eddie chuckled. "I didn't think so."

The waiter came over with their tickets and Steven lifted one hand, gesturing to her. "I'm getting those," he said, flicking his fingers in the air. She gave the lot to him, grinning widely.

"Here you go, sir." She turned and left the table with a glance over her shoulder at Steven.

Molly wondered if he'd been in there before.

"I'm paying for the food," Steven announced, holding up the tickets with a credit card under his thumb, "but you all are responsible for the tip. So fork it over, people. She did a great job with a crowd like us."

The rest of them agreed, and money was produced. Molly pulled a ten from her accordion wallet and tossed it on the pile growing in the middle of the table. By her estimation, she calculated the waitress would get about a fifty or sixty dollar tip.

Eddie took hold of her arm as she made to stand up. She looked at him curiously.

"I was wondering," he said quietly, "if you'd like to take a walk through downtown with me. I find it very soothing, especially after a good meal."

She could see he was anxious about asking. She was also fairly sure her anxiety level matched his at that point. She nodded. "I'd like that, yeah. Should we leave our cars here?"

"I think that would be safest, don't you? They don't close till one and we'll be back long before then. It's not even ten yet. Let's not make it a workout."

She giggled at his joke.

Molly walked next to Eddie, clutching her purse strap with one hand, wishing he would take the other and hold it.

Two days she had known the man, and she wanted to hold his hand. She wondered if he would pull his hand away. She'd had a boyfriend for a short period of time who always jerked away as if he hated to hold hands. He wasn't a very nice guy anyway, so it was no real loss to her when they broke up.

She pushed the thoughts away when she stepped out into the crisp night air. At first, she thought it might be too cold. But despite the low temperature, there was virtually no wind at all. It made the cool temperature tolerable, though she did stop at her car and get her coat.

"It's been so warm lately," Eddie said, helping her on with the jacket. She accepted his help and was aware that he was doing the "gentlemanly" thing the whole time he was doing it. He seemed to take it in stride. It was no big deal to him that he was helping her on with her jacket, holding it for her and adjusting it afterward to make sure it was on correctly and comfortably.

That was something Molly associated with people in a relationship.

That was silly, of course. After all, men were supposed to help a lady on with her jacket, weren't they? These days? Nah.

Molly snorted out loud, catching Eddie off guard. He widened his eyes, and she broke into a sharp laugh.

"I am so sorry. I was thinking about something…"

He laughed with her as she explained and replied, "I understand. I've done that."

They headed for the sidewalk outside the restaurant. Molly glanced across the street at the café where there had been "the sighting." She couldn't wait to see Vinnie in person herself. She wanted the man on the video to be him. She didn't want to do any more searching for unusual suspicious things or worry about being attacked by a vicious predator.

Eddie's description didn't make it seem like Vinnie was a monster.

But in her mind, the blip of the man on the screen for so short a time, wearing his black hoodie and grey sweatpants… the vision wouldn't go away. He *was* a monster. He sabotaged other people's property and threatened them.

He needed to be caught. Molly wanted him caught. Before he could do anything to her or anyone else she cared about.

Molly walked close by Eddie's side, wondering if he noticed she was doing that. She'd lifted both her hands and had them balled up in front of her. They were warmer when pressed against her jacket.

"If you're too cold, we can stop. You can go home. You don't have to—"

He stopped when she halted in place and turned to him. She looked up into his hazel eyes and smiled. "I'm fine, Eddie. Let's talk. I want to know about you. I want to hear about your likes and dislikes and all those things people put in their profiles."

Eddie looked doubtful. "I don't know what to tell you. Didn't we meet that first night to talk? I told you a lot about me then."

"But I want to know more. Did you grow up here in Virginia? What was it like? What were you like as a child? What's your favorite color? I don't care. I just want to know who you are. We'll be working close together and I'll be honest, Eddie. I'd like to know the person Steven seems so quick to trust. He's a good judge of character and if he trusts you to be the head of the online presence, you must be a really great guy."

Eddie blushed, which she thought was cute.

"I guess he just saw something in me," Eddie said, shrugging. "I'm your basic thirty-eight-year-old. Nothing special. Been a bachelor all my life, grew up in a foster home with a bunch of other kids on a farm. It was nice. Nice foster parents. The Lawlers, didn't make us work or anything like that. I mean, we had chores and the like, but nothing like work-work."

Molly nodded. "Right."

They had continued walking and were about to pass the library when she saw a man emerge from the alleyway beside the building and head in the same direction they were going. Something about the way he walked gave Molly a strange feeling.

She grabbed Eddie's arm. "Hey," she said, "is that Vinnie?"

Chapter Fourteen

Eddie squinted to focus on the retreating back of the tall man. He was surprised by how easily Molly pointed out the man, despite only having seen grainy video images. He nodded at her.

"Looks like him from behind. Come on. Let's see where he's going."

Eddie grabbed Molly's hand without thinking, leading her across the street, looking both ways before doing so. There were a few cars on the road, probably going home after a long day and a nice dinner out with friends, like they'd had. At least that's what he hoped for the people he saw. It was a happy thought, and he liked to hold on to those when he had them. Especially when he was dragging a woman along to pursue a man who could possibly be dangerous.

Eddie's suspicions when talking to the man hadn't gone any further than him being a reporter. Even now, it was hard to believe Vinnie was responsible for the frightening texts Molly was receiving. He had to wonder, too, why it was Molly who was targeted.

He glanced at her quickly but returned his gaze to the man in front of him, not wanting to lose sight of him. Foot traffic was light, but that didn't mean Vinnie might not turn abruptly and go a different way. "How did you know that was him? You've never seen his face, have you?"

Molly shook her head, her eyes steady on the man they were going after. "No, I never have."

"Maybe he knows you and that's why he's targeting you. Even though I got the impression he was interested in the entire Inn. I don't recall anyone but Steven being mentioned, and that was only because he's the owner."

He saw her look at him out of the corner of his eye. "I... I don't think he knows me. He doesn't look familiar to me from behind. Or in the videos. I don't know why I'm the one he's messaging. I don't even know if he's the one who's doing it."

"Are you the only one who's gotten any?" Eddie asked, slowing his pace when Vinnie did.

"No, there's—" A moment of panic struck him when it looked like Vinnie might turn around. If he did, he would definitely recognize Eddie and if he was after Molly, he would surely recognize her, too, even if she didn't recognize him.

The moment of fear for their safety made him abruptly turn and push Molly into an inverted store front. It would be better to lose sight of Vinnie than be seen by him. Eddie was sure of that.

He waited a moment, his hand covering Molly's mouth, his body pressed against hers. Then he pulled back and peeked around the wall. Vinnie had started walking again.

He didn't realize what he'd done until he looked back at Molly, his mouth open to tell her it was safe to continue after Vinnie. The expression on her face stopped him in his tracks. He lifted his eyebrows, pulling gently on the hand he had never let go of.

"I am so sorry, Molly. Did I scare you? I shouldn't have done that. I apologize."

"No... no..." Molly was shaking her head and when she spoke, her voice was breathless. "I was... I was taken by surprise but... I'm okay... I just wasn't expecting to be body crushed today, that's all."

Eddie was instantly relieved by her humor and grinned widely. He nearly said he would be glad to do it again if she liked it, but that seemed to forward. The fact he'd done it in the first place now felt incredibly forward of him.

"I now know the lengths to which you will go to keep me safe," she said in a firm voice, as if there was only the silver lining to think about. "So, thank you. Now let's go before we lose him."

This time it was Molly who pulled on his hand and rushed around the side of the building, looking first to make sure Vinnie was still in sight.

He had made it across another block by the time they finished their short chat and they had to jog to catch up.

"Shoot," Eddie murmured when Vinnie turned and disappeared behind a building. He shared a glance with Molly, who nodded as she let go of his hand. He was right behind her as she took off in a dead run, much to the surprise of a couple walking peacefully in the other direction.

Molly halted at the corner where Vinnie had turned off and peeked around into the alleyway. She looked over her shoulder at him, nodding.

"He's down there. Come on."

"Wait!" Eddie grabbed her arm. He looked around the corner and shuddered at the sight of the dark alleyway. He lowered his voice to a whisper and got closer to her. Even while he was speaking to her and focusing on her, he was also concentrating on what was going on around them. He was suddenly feeling the dangerous elements of what they were doing a lot more than before.

"I trust my instincts," he said quickly, "and I don't think this is a good idea. We've followed him to a bad area, an area I don't trust. We need to leave. We don't belong here."

He was glad Molly didn't make a fuss about it. In fact, she nodded curtly, turned on her heel and went back in the direction they'd come from. Once again, he found himself hurrying after her.

"Well, that was easy," he said when they got back to where the street was well-lit and there were other people around them.

Molly's face was rife with tension when she turned her face to him.

"I want to go home. We shouldn't have gone after him. I wish I hadn't even seen him."

"At least now you know who you're looking for. You saw his face this time, didn't you?"

"Not full on. But I won't forget his stance. I won't forget the way he walks." Her voice was so soft. Eddie's heart melted listening to it. He wished he knew just the right words to comfort her because that near-encounter seemed to have depleted her and upset her terribly.

"You're safe now, Molly."

"I don't know for how long, though," Molly countered. He heard the strain in her words. "What if he knows where I live?"

"Molly." Eddie turned her to him and looked deep into her worried eyes. "We don't even know if Vinnie is the one sending the texts. We might have just watched him coming back from the store or dinner alone to a hovel, a dump, the only place he can afford, probably. It could easily be pure coincidence that he was asking about the Inn, and that I had these suspicions about him."

"But he *is* the one on the video footage," Molly replied. "And he signed into the Inn twice as a guest! How do you explain that?"

"He didn't say he's never been there, Moll," Eddie countered. "In fact, he professes to love the place and see potential in it. For all we know, he might be a real estate developer and thinks the land is worth more than Steven is willing to put into it. Maybe he wants to invest."

Molly tilted her head. "You don't seriously think someone living or even going to a place like that would be involved in real estate, do you?"

Eddie had to admit that was a stretch. But he had to shake his head and continue, "Okay, so he's probably not a real estate developer. Doesn't mean he's the one sending you those texts." A thought struck him and he said, "Hey, you never told me who else has been getting texts. It sounded like you said there was someone else before. Did you?"

Molly nodded. He noticed she was walking at a steady, hard pace back to the restaurant parking lot. He matched it, though he wished their peaceful walk and talk hadn't been interrupted by Vinnie's appearance. She'd been relaxed and happy. Now she was tense, upset, possibly angry at him and not wanting to say it.

"One of the other girls in the administrative department got them before I did. She was managing several accounts and quit because of the harassment. She was terrified, and I understood that. We were all very worried when she didn't come in that day. But I got a text from her later explaining that she just didn't feel comfortable coming back and we sent her a severance package and everything. I haven't heard from her since."

Eddie lifted his eyebrows. "How long ago was that?"

Molly appeared to think about it. "I guess it's been about three weeks since she left," she replied. "Teresa was her name. Teresa Knox."

Chapter Fifteen

All Molly wanted to do at that point was go home. It had been a long day, a longer week, and she was ready to relax. One more workday left and the weekend would be upon them. She'd been pondering going to see Andy in North Carolina one weekend this month, but it would have to wait. She was anxious to know what might happen with Eddie and didn't want to leave at what might be a crucial stage in their relationship. Initially, she'd thought it would be nice to get away from the stress she was under from the threats on top of losing Teresa's help in the admin department.

Eddie seemed anxious to continue the night. As much as she wanted to go home, when she saw Steven's car was still at the restaurant, she looked over her shoulder at him. He met her eyes with a curious expression.

"Steven is still here," she said. "Let's go inside and talk to him."

Eddie nodded.

It had gotten nippier outside. Molly was relieved when she stepped inside the building and a warm rush of air met her face. She closed her eyes briefly before hurrying back to the table they'd left earlier. She stopped when she saw there was a different group of people occupying it.

"Molly!" Her name was being called softly through the quiet hum of the still bustling restaurant. She turned back to Eddie, who was gesturing toward the U-shaped bar in the middle of the lobby. Steven and Jack were there, sitting atop tall stools, facing each other slightly. They seemed to be having an intense conversation.

She crossed to where they were seated and came up behind them, clearing her throat so they would know she was there. They both turned to look at her.

"Ah, Molly," Steven said, straightening his spine and spinning on the stool. "Thought you'd gone home."

"Eddie and I went for a walk," she replied, moving her eyes from Steven to Jack. Both averted their eyes to give Eddie a single nod of acknowledgement. "We were just coming back, and I saw your car still here, Steven. Everything all right?"

Steven shrugged. "Yeah, we were just talking about all the stuff that's been happening."

Molly took the strap of her purse from her shoulder and slung the bag onto the bar as she sat on the stool next to Steven. Both men turned in her direction as Eddie sat on her other side. She faced away from him but gave him a glance so he'd know she knew he was there.

"Eddie and I just saw Vinnie," she said, "walking through downtown. He went to a very secluded and dark area where a lot of crime happens, if you know what I mean."

Steven frowned. "So you followed him?" He and Jack shared incredulous looks. "That was pretty dangerous, don't you think?"

"We didn't let him see us," Molly said, ignoring the irritation that made her chest tight. Didn't Steven understand how terrified she was of these threats? How badly she wanted it all to be resolved or just simply go away? "Eddie made sure he didn't. And when we saw where he was going, he pulled me away and we came back."

"I think we need to be careful about jumping to the conclusion that he's the one who's sending the texts," Eddie said, leaning forward more so all three of them could see him. In reaction, Molly sat back a little, so she wasn't in his way. He gave her a gentle look that quashed all her irritation. "I know you're afraid, Moll," he said softly. "I know you want this figured out and fixed so that you can go back to living a peaceful life. I really do understand that. I just want to be cautious. Accusing someone of these threats might ruin his life if he's innocent. We don't want to do that, do we?"

Molly blinked at him, wondering if he really thought there was a chance it wasn't Vinnie sending the texts. "Why do you trust him?" she asked, keeping her voice even. She saw out of the corner of her eye when Steven and Jack, who had been looking at her, both moved their eyes to Eddie.

"It's not that I trust him," Eddie replied without hesitation. "It's that I don't trust us not to jump to conclusions because of circumstantial evidence. I'm not a lawyer and I won't pretend to be one. But you have to think about defamation lawsuits and things like that because you don't want to dig a hole deeper than you can get out of. And if we go and get convinced that he's the guilty party now when he isn't, that means the real threat is still out there lurking and we aren't even *looking*."

He finished what he was saying with his eyes on Steven. Molly knew he was right. She was being threatened but it would be the Inn and Steven who would suffer if they pursued Vinnie without cause. And jumping to the wrong conclusion did leave the real threat still out there on her doorstep.

"I wasn't going to take out an op-ed," she responded, a little annoyed that Eddie was right, "but I... I see what you're saying.

I just think it's too much of a coincidence for these strange things to be happening and for him to be popping up on the CCTV right when the texts start coming. And he didn't stop when Teresa left. He moved to me. I still don't know why."

"Has anyone checked the employee records?" Jack asked casually. Steven, Molly, and Eddie all looked at him. He lifted his shoulders. "I mean, maybe this Vinnie guy used to work here. It would sure open up a lot more info about him. Even if it isn't current, it's a start, right?"

"I don't think he worked for me," Steven said, looking contemplative. "I interview everyone who is hired at the Inn. Everyone. From the next member of the board to the housekeepers. I get at least one interview with them. And I don't remember the man I saw on that video. I know it wasn't much to go by but I feel like I'd remember someone that tall and lanky. And what job would he possibly have had? He didn't tell Eddie he used to be an employee."

"It's a good idea, though, Jack," Molly put in, wanting her friend to know she appreciated his input. "I think we should at least run his name through the database and see what comes up. I'll do that tomorrow morning when I go in. He might have worked here years ago, and it was Ben who hired him."

"Of course you are right, Moll. I'm going to do some research, too." Steven pushed himself from the stool and took his coat from the back of it. He slung it around his shoulders as he spoke. "Jack, keep an eye out at the boatyard and see if this character comes back. I'm going to speak to the fellas at the police department and see if they'll run that number through. It's probably a burner phone, but we should find out, at least."

He stretched out both arms and locked his elbows, gripping the edge of the bar with his hands. "I'm a little ashamed, guys," he said in a sheepish tone.

He got the attention of the other three with that. Molly gazed at him sympathetically as he spoke.

"We should have taken Teresa more seriously. Her leaving so abruptly tells me we didn't do all we could. She didn't feel safe. I'll bear the burden for that." He shook his head, pushing to stand straight again.

"We did all we could, Steven," Molly said firmly, remembering what they'd gone through for their employee to work with her and help her figure out who her stalker was. That's what they'd thought at the time, anyway.

"We did." Jack backed her up. "Don't feel guilty. There was nothing more we could have done."

Chapter Sixteen

Molly tapped the button mindlessly, staring at the video playing out in front of her eyes. It was more footage of the boatyard. What she was watching was from the weekend. She was aware she was looking for a tall, lanky man in possibly a sweat suit. But her mind was not on the screen or what she was seeing. She was thinking about Eddie.

It had been four days since they'd seen him downtown after their dinner with the gang. She and Eddie didn't speak over the weekend, and she found herself wishing she had gone to see Andy after all.

But she didn't and now it was Monday again and she was staring at the monitor because she had nothing better to do.

First thing that morning, she'd texted Steven to see if he'd had any progress over the weekend. His main goal, he'd told her, was to find out where Teresa went. He'd wanted to ask her if she'd continued receiving threats after she left or if the texter had immediately switched to Molly. He'd had a long list of questions for her, Molly remembered.

But Steven hadn't found Teresa. He said no one answered at her home or her cell. The mailbox outside her home was so stuffed with mail some had fallen on the ground and the mailman started piling it up directly in front of the screen door.

She went over what he'd told her in her mind, trying to figure out why Teresa would up and leave town without taking care of her mail or her house. She'd asked him if Teresa's blue Jetta was in the driveway and he'd said yes. It was.

Was Teresa really so scared that she'd just up and left? Had she simply packed a bag, got a taxi to the airport, and left the state or even the country entirely?

As she clicked the button to make the video pause and unpause or go faster or slower, another idea came to her mind. Maybe the threats stopped after Teresa left the Inn and she was still so upset about it, she started texting Molly as some sort of revenge?

A million things floated through Molly's mind, but none of them gave her any solid reason why anyone would target her. The worst thing about it was that for once in her life, she felt she could be open and honest with a man in a way that wouldn't feel completely awkward.

In one week, Eddie had shown her the kind of attention she'd desired her entire life. He wasn't over the top, but he was impulsive. There was no fear when he was around. She didn't consider her nervousness actual fear. She felt like it was logical for her to be nervous, worried that she would say the wrong thing and look silly.

Why had he come when she was in such a strange, mysterious, and dangerous situation?

Molly tapped her finger some more. There was no one in the VT room except her, so she wasn't annoying anyone but herself. She grunted, pursing her lips when she saw a shadow figure emerge from the very same place he had been before.

It was definitely Vinnie. There was no mistaking him this time. Her breath caught in her throat and she leaned so close to the screen her nose was almost touching. She narrowed her eyes, pulling back a bit.

"There you are," she growled. No matter what Eddie thought, Molly was sure Vinnie was the one sending the text messages. He might have seemed friendly to Eddie. Maybe just a bit nosy, poking around the Inn where he shouldn't have been poking around, but Molly saw him in a different light.

The grounds around the boatyard and the entire Inn itself were Steven's property. But people had been exploring since the place was built. They'd been digging holes, children had probably buried pets. There was no rule that said the land couldn't be explored.

So what Vinnie was doing wasn't against the law. Molly sighed heavily, realizing Steven was right. Vinnie could skulk around and look as creepy as he wanted. But until he dug something up and took it off Steven's land, he wasn't stealing or breaking any laws.

Molly watched him move across the pier where he'd come out of the woods. He walked along the edge of the water once he left the pier behind, not turning back. His head was down. His eyes were on the ground.

What was he looking for?

Molly rotated the ball on her mouse, zooming in on the video as much as she could without making it impossible to see what was going on. Her eyes dropped to the sand below Vinnie's feet.

At one point, Vinnie appeared to see something. He halted in place. His head stayed down for a moment or two before he dropped to his knees.

Fascinated, Molly stared at the screen, barely wanting to blink. She didn't want to miss anything. If he took something from the property, she would have something to report him for. That would be theft. And if he wasn't the one sending the threats, it would be found out and he would just have to pay a small fine and give back whatever he took.

But that's not how Molly felt it would turn out.

"What's there, Vinnie?" she mumbled. "What do you see?"

Vinnie dug in the ground with a small trowel he'd taken from the backpack he had slung around his shoulders. He set the trowel aside after a few digs and used his hands to brush the sand away from whatever he was digging out.

Molly held her breath. What was it? She instinctively sat forward again since the video was zoomed in as far as she could get it.

Finally, Vinnie stood up, taking a triumphant stance. He brushed the object in his hand off but it was heavy so he couldn't take many swipes before he had to use both hands to hold it up.

Molly could tell it was heavy because he hefted it under one arm as he slung the backpack around his shoulder again and started to walk away.

She stared at the large oval-shaped object until she realized what he'd found.

It was a rock. A perfectly egg-shaped rock, but it was still nothing more than a rock.

Molly gritted her teeth and sat back in her chair so hard it moved back a few inches on its wheels. "A rock! Are you serious!"

She shoved the mouse away from her and used one hand to hold her chin while she continued to stare at the screen. The man was walking away. He'd done nothing wrong, once again.

How was she going to prove he was responsible for the threats against her if he was going to continue to uphold the law?

Molly swung around in her chair when she heard the door open behind her. It was Eddie.

A rush of warmth spread through her. She smiled at him, her frustration taking a back seat.

"Eddie," she said. "I didn't know when I would see you this morning. Did you have a good weekend?"

Eddie lifted his eyebrows, his eyes on the monitor behind her. "I did," he responded as he came over, taking the seat next to her and leaning toward the monitor the way she'd been doing a few minutes before. "It was kind of boring, though."

He was so close to her when he turned his head to give her a friendly look, it sent tingles through her. "I didn't really have anyone to talk to except Jackson."

Molly gave him a curious look. She hadn't realized he had a roommate. She wondered what that must be like at his age. It would seem the roommate age would be long gone by thirty-eight.

"Jackson?"

Eddie grinned widely, moving his hand to the mouse she'd flung away from herself and pulling it back. "Yeah. Jerry Jackson, Jr. My talking parrot."

Molly raised one eyebrow. "Nuh-uh." She laughed. "You do not have a talking parrot."

Eddie looked affronted. "I most certainly do."

"Can I meet him sometime?"

Eddie chuckled. "I'll ask Steven if there's a 'bring your pet to work' day."

Molly laughed with him. She was thinking she'd rather visit him at his place than have him bring the bird to work.

Chapter Seventeen

"Look," Eddie said, drawing Molly's attention away from him and to the monitor again. She averted her eyes and was immediately fascinated by what he was pointing out on the screen.

"That's Steven," she said, softly, peering at the perfectly clear video they were watching. "Is this now?" She moved her eyes to the timestamp on the lower left-hand side of the screen. It was running in real time.

"Yeah. That's Jack, look. He's coming out of the boat shelter with... what's that? A shovel?"

"Two shovels," Molly replied. She reached out and flipped the button to turn the monitor off. "Let's go see what they're doing."

Eddie looked excited by the prospect. He was back on his feet behind her and they left the VT room behind.

The air outside was pleasant. Molly enjoyed the Springtime months in Virginia. She breathed in especially deep, thanking God for creating such a gorgeous day. They left through one of the back entrances that took them around the kitchens and the housekeeping areas. Molly watched several employees moving back and forth, dodging them to get to the sidewalk that curled down around the golf course. It was a small nineteen-hole course that was there when they first arrived and was much more plush and green now than it had been then.

She almost stopped and got a golf cart to drive down in, but decided against it at the last minute. She didn't want to draw any attention to what she and Eddie—or Steven and Jack, for that matter—were doing.

While they jogged down the curving sidewalk, she kept her eyes on the woods beyond the boatyard, keeping watch for Vinnie. He'd been there over the weekend. If she looked hard enough, she could probably find the oval-shaped hole where the rock was that he removed.

Was it theft to remove a large rock from someone else's property?

She wasn't going to ask. She would just have to wait for something more substantial to put him in jail, where she was sure he belonged.

She didn't see him and soon they were walking along the planks that began at the little shop and rental store Jack ran and went all the way to the beginning of the shore. There was a stretch of beach, but no one was out there. It was still a little early for swimmers, being the first weeks of May. In less than thirty days, there would be daily swimmers, coming to enjoy fun in the water.

Molly squinted to focus better on what Steven and Jack were doing. They were at the very edge of the rock wall that kept the land at the end of the pier, where it met the water from toppling in during heavy storms. They were dangerously close to the edge. If they continued to dig where they were digging, there was a good chance the pier structure would be compromised.

And Steven, not a small man himself, was on the side of the pier that could easily fall into the water.

"What in heaven's name are you two doing?" she demanded as they got closer, allowing some amusement in her voice so they would know she wasn't being hateful.

Steven looked up at her. "There's treasure down here," he stated plainly, as if he'd just told her he was planting tomatoes. His eyes moved back to the hole Jack was currently digging.

Molly and Eddie shared a glance.

"Okay, Steven, I'll bite," Molly said softly. "What's going on? What are you talking about?"

"Well, remember how Eddie here said Vinnie said the land needed to be explored more? That he wanted to explore it? I did some digging of my own." He turned his eyes to Jack, who glanced up in time to meet his friend's eyes. "No pun intended, Jack."

Jack shook his head, letting out a sharp chuckle. "You dug it before me, Steven. I'm not gonna complain."

Steven stood up and met Eddie and Molly a few feet away from their digging spot. He pulled a small paperback out of the large pocket of his jacket and handed it to her.

"Take a look at this."

Molly stared at the front cover of the book in her hands. It was titled "Lost Treasures of Virginia." She turned it over instinctively and scanned the back. It was a book filled with different anecdotes about treasures buried all over the state of Virginia, most of them near the coast.

"You found the Inn in here?" she asked, holding the book up.

Steven nodded, his eyes skirting to Eddie. "And you need to look at that, Eddie. Right there." Steven reached over and pointed at the book in Molly's hands. She looked down to see his finger was just above the name of the author.

Chills ran up her spine.

"Sabatino LaBrock," she read it aloud in a stunned voice.

"What?" Eddie's retort was sharp. He snatched the book from her hands and read the name himself. Molly didn't mind that he grabbed it from her. She probably would have done the same thing.

"That's the same last name as Vinnie," she remarked, knowing she was speaking the obvious.

"Yes," Steven said, nodding, "and look at chapter four. That's the Inn. There's even a map in there. But just of the property. Like a blueprint. It doesn't have an x marks the spot on it or anything. So we decided to do a little deducing of our own. Right, Jack?"

Jack looked up at Steven. "Yeah," he replied, jabbing the shovel down and dropping his eyes to the dirt he was digging into.

Steven took the book from Eddie's hands and turned so he could show them the book while standing beside them. He opened it to a page that was dog-eared.

"Where did you find this book, Steven?" Molly asked, amazed that such a thing even existed and that Steven had managed to find it.

"Apparently there's a little library room in the Inn," Steven replied, lifting his eyebrows. He looked as surprised as Molly at that revelation. "I never even knew about it. It's been closed off, in one of the wings we haven't touched because of money concerns. The books are still all in there on the shelves. It's really neat, like walking into a time capsule full of books. You'll love it, Molly."

Molly's heart raced at the thought. She wanted to be in that room right at that moment. Her excitement would have to wait, though, as there were more pressing matters right at that moment.

"This book was among them. Look at it right here. This talks about trees and structures that were here fifty years ago, when this book was written. It doesn't look the same now. See?" From another pocket, he pulled out a small map with a more familiar outline to Molly than the one in the book.

"Well, what do you know!" she exclaimed, moving her eyes from one to the other. "I see it now!"

Steven nodded, a look of satisfaction on his face. "So I did a little restructuring and came up with this spot right here. The treasure, if there is any, should be down here."

"What are you going to do if you don't find the treasure there?" Molly asked, curiously, turning her eyes to Jack, who was looking weary as he constantly rammed his shovel against the thick, solid rock wall when he was attempting to get dirt instead. "You're gonna break your wrists, Jack. And if you guys keep digging in that dirt, it's gonna give way, and the pier is gonna fall in on that side. If you keep digging, don't go back out on the pier, Steven. It's going to fall in. I guarantee it."

Steven nodded. "We'll be careful."

Chapter Eighteen

Eddie was amused by what Steven and Jack were doing. If someone had told him a few months ago he'd be watching his boss and coworkers dig for buried treasure and that he'd actually be *excited* about it, he would have told them they were crazy.

But here it was, actually happening.

And he was loving it.

"I saw Vinnie on the video footage from this weekend," Molly said, stepping away from the edge of the pier. He could see from the look on her face she was sure it was going to give way before they stopped digging. He skirted to the side, too, to show solidarity with her. She grinned at him and he knew she knew what he'd done.

In that moment, Eddie realized that was the first time he'd ever felt a real kinship with someone else. He hadn't even had any friends in his past where he'd been able to look at them and know what they were thinking.

"Oh, will you please stop digging right there?" Molly said, her tense voice a bit fearful.

Jack hopped away from the hole, acting as though it was on the verge of collapsing the pier into the water.

"I think she's probably right, Steven," he said, amusement in his voice. "I better put this dirt back. There's no buried treasure right here. Maybe we should get some metal detectors."

Steven's eyebrows shot up. He was considering it. Eddie was delighted by what he was watching. These three had obviously been around each other for so long, they were one hundred percent comfortable with each other. There wasn't even a moment of tension between them. He was amazed and fascinated by it at the same time.

"Metal detectors, huh? I bet I could find those online. Some good ones. Not cheap ones."

Jack whipped his phone out of his back pocket, leaning the shovel against his waist. Steven shoved the book toward Molly, who took it and tucked it under her arm. She turned and looked down at Steven's phone with him.

"Let's see..." Steven murmured as he tapped on the keyboard. "Metal... detectors... Yeah, look at that. We could drive out and get two of them right now."

"You guys really don't have any work to do?" Molly asked, grinning at the two of them.

Eddie had to laugh when Steven and Jack just stared at the woman before turning away and talking excitedly about which one they wanted to buy, comparing what they saw on their phones.

He held out one hand to her when she turned wide eyes to him, her eyebrows raised.

"Did you see what they just did to me?" she asked, as if she was stunned by it. She did take his hand, though, much to his delight.

"I did. And it was truly shameful. Come on. I'll buy you some ice cream and make you feel better."

Molly grinned from ear to ear, sending a satisfying warmth through Eddie. "I don't want ice cream. That's cold. But you can buy me some nachos. That would hit the spot."

Eddie laughed. "Nachos, it is! Almost lunch time anyway."

Molly shook her head, turning her naked wrist up to her eyes. "Oh, it's a bit early, but you know, it's really never too early for nachos."

"It looks like you're feeling a little better. Are you?" He hoped so. She'd been looking pretty aggravated when he first arrived at the VT room. He'd searched the building for her before realizing where she was. He'd even asked Steven (apparently before his boss and Jack went out to dig for buried treasure) and was told Molly hadn't been seen.

He wondered how early she'd gotten there that morning. He also wondered if she'd done anything that weekend and wished they'd spent it together. Jackson had always made such a great companion. But now that Molly was in the picture, his bird best friend just didn't satisfy him as much as it used to. He longed for human companionship now. A specific human.

"I guess it makes me feel better knowing that Vinnie is probably after that buried treasure," Molly continued. "I still don't know why he would choose to harass me. I have no idea what I did to him. But if that's what he's after and Steven is after the same thing, I have my odds on Steven, since this is his property. He grew up coming here and knows it like the back of his hand. He's walked this land for the last five years. He'll find it and Vinnie will back off, and I won't feel so threatened anymore."

Eddie wasn't as convinced as Molly. He was glad she was feeling better and more confident. But he wasn't entirely sure Vinnie was even the person behind the threatening texts. If he wasn't, that meant the threat would continue whether Steven found the treasure or not.

Although he wanted to say something about it right then, he didn't want to destroy her good mood. So he kept quiet and followed her back up the winding path to the Inn.

"This really is beautiful land, isn't it?" he remarked, stopping halfway up the hill to look out over the water. The inlet was flanked on both sides with stretches of land that went out at least half a mile on both sides before turning to create tall ledges along the water's edge that grew taller and taller until they were well above the surface.

The water was incredibly blue. The sand on the shore nearly sparkled as if it was made of crystals. Grass on both sides of the sidewalk all along the hillside was as green as grass could ever be. He hadn't taken the time to really look at it before. It was impressive.

"Yes, it is beautiful," Molly agreed, also stopping to take in the picture around her. "I've always loved it. Never expected to get a chance to actually live here, though. It's pretty amazing. People say you get used to living in beautiful places, like at the beach or deep in the woods, but I've never stopped enjoying how nice it is here. I love Virginia weather. Always have."

Eddie was about to remark on the landscape being almost as beautiful as she was when they were interrupted by a tinkling sound. Without thinking, Molly pulled her phone from her pocket and pressed her finger against the side to open it with her print.

He watched her face as she read the text she'd received. He was dismayed to see her good mood deflate and disappear. The corners of her lips turned down, and she flipped the phone around so he could read it.

"*You're next*," he read it aloud. He frowned, turning his eyes to hers. "You're next? What does that mean? Who was first?"

"That's the million-dollar question. Maybe he means Teresa. She was receiving texts before me. But what does he mean by I'm next? And I was thinking earlier... what if Teresa is mad about the way the texts were handled and is taking it out on me now? Maybe these are coming from her. I know it's far-fetched, but..." She shrugged.

"Not really. It is kind of strange that Steven couldn't find her and that all that mail had piled up like that. She's obviously not there and hasn't been for at least a couple weeks. That's a lot of mail and people don't even get that much anymore."

Where had the woman gone?

"I think we better try to find her, at least. And we have to warn Steven. If he's getting close to that treasure and Vinnie has done something to Teresa, he needs to know the man will go to any lengths."

Eddie was almost glad the text had come at that point. If it put Molly back on her guard—even if she was going after a man who could very well be innocent—it was a good thing for her to be prepared and watchful.

Molly turned and headed back down to where Steven and Jack were now sitting on a set of steps, both looking at their phones. Eddie wished he'd gotten out his compliment before the text had come. He would have liked to see the pretty blush come to her cheeks.

It would have to wait till next time. He planned to tell her what he was feeling and thinking and when he finally did, he would keep telling her until she told him to stop.

Chapter Nineteen

Eddie couldn't sleep. He stared up at the ceiling; the mystery surrounding Vinnie, the hidden treasure, and the threatening texts. He'd inadvertently put himself in the middle of it when Vinnie overheard his conversation with Emily. He had put a face to the mysterious man on the video.

Thinking back to the café and talking to Vinnie, he still couldn't convince himself the man was responsible for the texts. He could think of a number of possibilities that could explain everything.

Molly seemed to be acquainted pretty well with Teresa Knox, the woman who vanished into thin air. What if Molly's theory that Teresa was the one behind it all was actually the case? What if the two situations were oddly intertwined only because they were happening at the same time?

Could it be a coincidence?

Eddie frowned in the darkness. Why would Teresa pull of such a strange stunt? Texting herself or having someone text her, quitting, and texting Molly instead? What was the point?

Eddie dismissed the theory. Molly was right. It was too farfetched.

It was more likely Teresa had absconded as quick as she could to get away from whatever danger was posed to her.

Maybe that was the goal of the latest text message "You're next."

Whoever it was might want Molly to quit, to leave the Inn. If she did, would the messages go out to the other heads of department? Would Steven receive them?

Eddie hated to think that anyone would threaten Steven or Jack. He'd grown to like the group of friends quite a lot. It was bad enough Molly was being threatened. He didn't want that threat to spread to the others.

Besides, Molly wasn't going anywhere. He was sure of that.

He turned over on his side and cupped his hands under his head. The digital clock by his bed displayed the numbers 3:42.

"Three o'clock is the witching hour, isn't it?" He didn't know. He slung the covers off his legs and slid out to sit up. With slumped shoulders, he pushed up and trudged to the bathroom door. It was cracked open and a sliver of light was coming through. Eddie didn't like to sleep in complete darkness. It was one thing his foster parents had insisted on and when Eddie was old enough to make his own decisions, he decided leaving a little bit of light for himself to see in the darkness wasn't a bad thing.

He wasn't afraid of the dark. He was afraid of tripping because he couldn't see.

Eddie slid his hand inside the door instead of pushing it open and flipped the switch to dim. He'd had the special light fixture installed so he wasn't blinded by the sudden brightness.

Five minutes later, he emerged from the bathroom and headed for the kitchen. He was fully awake now. There was no going back to sleep for him tonight.

He sat at the island bar in the middle of his kitchen on a tall stool and looked around. It wasn't a bad place for someone his age. Maybe a tad big for just him but that's why he liked it. The large rooms made him feel free to move about. The space wasn't restricted at all. He wasn't closed in.

He pushed himself to his feet and went to the fridge, pulling it open, blocking the light with his hand until his eyes were used to it. He scanned the inside and reached for a bottle of sweet tea. His eyes strayed to the covered bird cage as he twisted the top to open the bottle.

A strange sense of melancholy overwhelmed him.

Ever since he got Jackson Jr., he'd been talking to him every day, no matter what time of day it was. The bird was his best friend.

Now, the virtually one-sided conversation wasn't enough.

All Eddie could think was that he wished Molly was there to talk to.

He glanced at the side table by the couch in the living room, which was open to the kitchen area. He couldn't see it, but he knew his cell phone was there, sitting on the charger. It was four o'clock in the morning. He couldn't very well call her, could he?

Did he dare send a text?

Sighing, Eddie headed back to his room. On the way, he amused himself with thoughts of what he would have done if there were no cell phones. He could always write her note. Fold it up like a football and make her guess which hand it was in. He could put in a couple boxes with yes or no next to them and ask her if she like-liked him, too. That might get the ball rolling.

By the time he was back in his room, Eddie was chuckling uncontrollably. He'd never had a chance to give those kind of notes in school, especially not elementary school, when it was really the popular thing to do. Eddie didn't do anything that was popular. He wasn't in Band or Drama. He wasn't remarkable in anything, joined no clubs, didn't run for class president or prom king and he didn't stand out.

Just the way he liked it.

That led to what many people would have considered a very lonely existence. They didn't understand, though. Eddie liked it that way. While he wouldn't have said no to a chance at love and marriage during his nearly twenty years of being an independent adult, he wasn't about to put himself out there for consideration.

He'd grown up one of many children, first in the orphanage and then in the foster home. He wasn't seen then, and he didn't want to be seen now.

Except by Molly.

He wanted *her* to see him.

He sat on the edge of his bed and drank half the tea in the bottle. He still had it lifted and almost choked when the corner of his eye caught his phone lighting up in the living room through the open doorway. His heart gave a leap when he heard the vibration that soon followed.

Eddie was on his feet and at the phone before he could blink. He snatched it from the charger and stared at the screen. He'd received a text message.

"Please don't let it be spam," he murmured, unlocking the phone to view the message.

It was from Molly. He couldn't believe it. She was awake at the same time as him! Did he dare respond and let her know he'd seen it? Did she want to talk?

Hey, meet me at the café tomorrow where you saw Vinnie. I'll be there at 8. Steven already knows and you won't be docked for the time.

It was a completely impersonal and all business message. He could hear her voice saying the words to him.

He lowered the phone and then snatched it back up when it buzzed again. Another message had come through from her.

It says you read my message. Are you up? Respond if you are.

Eddie's heart went into overdrive. She wanted to talk to him. He wondered if she wanted to talk to him as much as he wanted to talk to her. He calmed himself and tapped out a response.

I'm up. Woke up wide awake. Can't get back to sleep. Why you up?

His eyes still down on the phone, excitement growing in his chest, he went back to his bedroom and hopped on the bed, propping one leg up while the other hung over the edge.

Same, came her response. *We should meet up for coffee or something.*

Eddie's eyebrows shot up. Was she asking him out?

We'll be at the café in less than four hours, he sent back. *I'm all for getting there early if you want but I don't think they'll be open right now.*

Eddie tried to picture her, but he'd never seen the inside of her suite and could only picture her in business clothes.

I guess we should try to get a couple more hours of sleep then, huh?

Eddie regretted it but agreed with her. Besides, if he could sleep, he would be seeing her a lot sooner.

Chapter Twenty

Eddie gave Emily a smile as soon as he entered the café. She smiled back but looked a bit confused when he went to the table where Molly was seated. Realization came to her face and another smile replaced the original one. Eddie knew exactly what that meant.

"Morning," he said, sliding into the booth opposite Molly, whose eyes were on the menu. Her eyes lifted to him.

"Morning," she responded. "Did you get any sleep after we talked this morning?"

"I did, actually." Eddie had even surprised himself by how comfortable he'd been after talking to her. "It was probably that tea. Helped me sleep. Had nothing to do with a breakfast date or anything."

Molly giggled. "Is that what this is? A breakfast date? Is it official?"

Eddie's chest tightened with apprehension. He dismissed it, seeing that she was teasing him.

"I am going to consider it one. I hope you will, too. Even if we do talk about business."

Molly shook her head, sliding the second menu she'd gotten over to him. "We aren't really going to, though. But don't tell Steven. I won't put this meal on my expense sheet, but he doesn't need to know what we're discussing. Besides, all we have to do is say something about the Inn and it's a business meal. Like..." She lifted her eyes to the ceiling to think. When she dropped them to his face again, he was so amused by the look of excitement there, he had to let out a chuckle. "Like, you know the account sheets that are due at the end of each week?" She reached down to the seat next to her where Eddie couldn't see and brought up a folder, which she slapped on the table. She tapped it with the back of her fingers. "There they are. Bam. Business meeting."

Eddie laughed just as Emily approached with a glass of water.

"Good morning, Eddie," the waitress said with a smile.

"Good morning, Emily," he replied. "How have you been?"

"Oh, I won't complain," the woman responded in a friendly voice. "I see you are enjoying your new job." She looked at Molly and winked mischievously. "Or are you here to fire him? I hope not. He's a pretty good guy from all I've seen."

Molly looked a little shocked and turned her eyes to Eddie. "I won't be firing Eddie, no," she said in a serious tone. "If you see him in here with our boss, Steven, then you might worry."

Eddie moved his eyes between the women. "What's happening here? Why is me being fired even being discussed?"

Both women laughed.

"What would you like for breakfast, Eddie?" Emily asked through her laughter. "I haven't seen you in here this early before. Always lunch. You want a burger for breakfast?"

He shook his head, pulling the menu closer. "Nah. And I'll have to look for a minute. I don't know what I want. Or what you even offer."

"Coffee?"

He nodded at her. "Yeah, with cream and sugar on the side, too."

Emily moved her eyes to the end of the table by the window, where the usual condiments were stacked in a little black tray with a round circle handle. He saw the eye gesture and glanced at the tray.

"Oh, yeah, of course. I will need the cream, though."

"Of course. I'll be right back, dear."

Emily spun around and hurried toward the kitchen to get his coffee.

"You come here a lot, then?" Molly asked, her eyes on the retreating waitress.

"A few times a week, yeah," Eddie replied, glancing around. "I guess I've become one of the regulars. My house is on the other side of Vinton, so I didn't start coming here until I got the job at the Inn. I've made friends with Emily."

"How often have you seen Vinnie? Are you still coming here that often?"

Eddie returned his eyes to her face. He didn't look at Emily when she set his coffee cup on the table with a small saucer of cream, but he did say "thank you." He didn't want to give Molly the impression there was more to his friendship with the waitress than there was.

He wanted to make it clear who he was interested in.

"I only saw him that one time last week. And then, of course, when we went walking downtown." He looked over at Emily, who was leaving the table. "Hey, Emily."

She turned and came back to the table, her eyebrows raised in curiosity.

"You remember that guy that came over and was talking to me about the Inn last week? He was saying how Steven hasn't explored it enough. You remember that?"

Emily nodded, crossing her arms over her chest. She looked at Molly. "I do remember him. Was he a friend of yours?"

"No," Molly said, her face crumpling in on itself. Her lips pinched, her brow furrowed, and her eyes dropped to the table. Even in that state, Eddie couldn't help thinking she looked like a wounded bunny rabbit.

"We think he might be behind some sabotage and trespassing at the Inn," Eddie hurried to say. "And Molly has been receiving some threatening texts that might possibly be from him." He hated to put it that way. He expected and received a hard look from Molly.

"We're trying to figure things out, that's all. Have you seen him in here since then?"

Emily appeared to think about it, lifting her eyes to the ceiling and making a humming noise. "Well, actually, I think he was in here once after that. It was at about the same time. He had lunch. Grilled cheese on rye with salsa and a side of tots."

"He was alone?" Molly asked.

Emily nodded. "Sure was."

"He didn't talk to anyone while he was here?" Eddie wondered what Molly was thinking. "Did he talk to you? Like when I was here and he talked to both of us. Was he friendly like that with you?"

"Well..." Emily spoke slowly. "I wouldn't say he was as friendly as that day, but he wasn't *not* friendly either. He smiled at me. I smiled at him. He complimented the food. Left me a five-dollar tip, which is more than most."

Molly and Eddie were quiet for a moment.

"Do you remember what he was doing while he was here?" Molly asked. "I mean, besides eating and drinking, of course. Did he have any books or documents with him? Maybe a map or anything like that?"

Eddie was impressed with Molly's questions. He gazed at Emily, anxious for the answers.

"Well..." Emily hesitated again. Eddie was glad she was giving it good thought. She wasn't dismissive, and that made a lot of difference. "He did have a book with him. I don't know the title. It had a red cover. Not a hardback. In fact, it was so soft, it looked almost like fabric. When he was reading one side, the other was just flopped over all limp, you know." She lifted one arm with her hand limp at the wrist. "It had a red fabric bookmark attached. A ribbon. You know what I mean?"

Eddie and Molly both nodded, sharing a look. The book written by Sabatino LaBrock had a red cover.

"Do you remember anything else about the time he spent here?" Molly persisted.

"I don't think so," Emily responded, "but I'll let you know if I think of anything."

"Thank you."

Emily nodded at Molly, swiveling her eyes to Eddie. "More coffee?"

"Yeah, I'll have a top-off, thank you."

The waitress moved off to get the coffee with both Eddie and Molly watching.

"She's a nice lady," Molly said. "I should come here more often."

"She's great, yeah. So we know that Vinnie has the LaBrock book now. I think it's safe to say he is looking for the treasure that Steven is looking for, too."

"We'll have to tell Steven about this. It really just confirms what we already suspected, but he definitely needs to be told."

"After breakfast?" Eddie asked, hope in his voice.

She grinned softly. "After breakfast."

Chapter Twenty-One

Crickets.

The little creatures were the only thing Molly heard when she opened her eyes. It was pitch dark.

Two days had passed since the breakfast date she'd had with Eddie. Since then Steven had continued to dig. No one heard from Vinnie or Teresa and the workdays seemed to meld together.

Molly didn't feel normal anymore. It felt like something was about to change drastically and she was just waiting for that phone call... that text...

Her heart jumped when her thoughts moved to the text messages she'd been getting. She rolled over and looked at her phone propped up on the stand that it charged on every night. It was lit up and a small icon showed her she had an unread text.

Molly didn't want to be wide awake again. The clock on the phone said it was 2:15, which was earlier and a better time to be woken up. It meant she could get more sleep when she finally did get to again.

That didn't comfort her, though, considering how wide awake she really was.

Molly kept her phone on silent at night so it wouldn't wake her up. The light usually didn't register in her brain or bother her. She sighed heavily as she reached for it. Maybe it was from Eddie. She didn't know whether a message from him would help her get back to sleep or hinder that from happening.

She unlocked the phone and pulled up the message.

LEAVE THE INN BEFORE YOU DIE. YOU ARE NEXT.

Molly sat up straight in bed and stared at the screen. She began an immediate prayer in her mind as her shaking fingers texted back to the unknown aggressor.

Who is this? Leave me alone! Stop messaging me!

When Molly hit send, she realized it was the first time she'd texted back. Her eyes lifted to the number of the sender. It was an email address, which always confused her. But this time, she spotted something she hadn't seen before.

The letters in the address got her attention. She was a little aggravated with herself for not having seen it before.

Before the at sign, the letter said 1SA.B.LABLLC.

She ran her eyes over the letters repeatedly, chills sliding over her arms and down her spine.

Sliding her legs out of the covers, she got out of bed and went closer to her window, where there was a lamp. She touched the bottom of the lamp to turn the light on its dimmest setting.

The double glass doors that led to her balcony were slightly open and the thin curtains were billowing out into the room. The breeze wasn't cold, so Molly didn't close the doors. Instead, she went to the glass doors and looked out at the water stretching out to the horizon in front of her.

Her eyes dropped to the boatyard when a flash of light caught her eye. Her heart went into overdrive when, at the same time, her phone lit up in her hand.

She looked down at the text message that had come through.

You will soon find out.

Terrified tears filled Molly's eyes. She backed away from the doors at first and then rushed to close them, as if somehow her tormentor was on the balcony, ready to pounce in and get her.

She hurried back to her bed, closing out the text message from the stranger and pulling up Eddie's number instead.

Are you up?

She hit send and waited with an anxious, beating heart. The box of tissues next to her bed would be empty by the time she was done mopping up her tears if he didn't hurry up and answer her back.

She got no response. Her heart sunk. The only other person she would dare bother at this time of night was Steven. Or maybe Paula or Jack.

But Molly wanted to talk to Eddie. She wanted his help. She wanted to hear his voice and listen to him comforting her, making her feel more secure. He didn't even have to be there. Just hearing his voice would be enough for her.

"Please, Father," she prayed softly. "Please comfort me and give me security. I'm so scared right now. I need Your help."

Her prayer was immediately answered when her phone lit up. This time, it wasn't a text message coming through. It was a call. And it was Eddie.

She answered it immediately.

"I'm so glad you called," she whispered into the phone.

"What's wrong, Molly?" Eddie asked, concern in his voice. "What's happened?"

"I got another message."

"A text?"

"Yes. Two of them. Because I responded."

Eddie was quiet for a moment. "You've never responded before?"

"No."

"Save the number in your phone. Don't delete the messages. You will need them when this guy is caught."

"I think it's Vinnie, Eddie," Molly said, keeping her voice low, her eyes moving between the door of her suite and the window. "I saw a light out at the boatyard and I haven't called anyone about it."

"What?" He sounded bewildered. "You need to call them right now, Molly. What are you thinking? He could be right outside your... call the police and Steven. I'm on my way right now."

"Edd—" He had hung up the phone before she could tell him she wasn't sure she'd seen anything more than a reflection out there. The most logical thing to do would be calling Steven, at least, and explaining things to him. The police weren't necessary.

And if Eddie wanted to come over because he was worried about her, who was she to stop him?

A glance at the clock told her it was just a bit past three in the morning. Molly looked at the double glass doors. She had a tight grip on her phone as she pondered whether or not to go over and see if the light was still there. She should probably at least determine it was real and a legitimate problem before she called in the authorities.

She took a few steps over and lifted up, bending forward. She still couldn't really see the boatyard.

Sighing, Molly realized she would have to go to the doors where she'd been before and look out. Otherwise, she simply couldn't see. And she needed to verify she'd actually seen something.

As soon as she stepped back to the place she'd been before, Molly saw the light again. This time, however, it was obviously a flashlight. It was weaving back and forth on the ground in a small area near the furthest pier from the rental shop.

Fear pierced her heart, but Molly pushed it down. The man with the flashlight was far, far away from her. He couldn't just start running and come get her. She was protected where she was, and wasn't even on the bottom floor anyway. He'd have to be Superman to get to her before she had time to stop him or do something about it.

She texted Eddie that the man with the light was still at the boatyard and she was safe. She would call Steven, but not the police unless he wanted her to. For all they knew, it could be Jack wandering around down there. That was his area of expertise, after all.

Then she called Steven.

The phone rang on the other end, but she didn't know if he kept his phone on silent the way she did. She pondered going over to his suite and waking him. It was important that someone check out who that was down at the boatyard, but calling the police still seemed extreme to Molly. They had no security guards as such at the Inn.

Maybe it was time for Steven to employ some.

She went to the door of her bedroom and flipped on the light switch next to it. She had to get dressed. It was probably best to get Steven up herself.

Chapter Twenty-Two

Eddie was out of bed the moment he got the text from Molly. Ever since they'd texted at 3:45 in the morning, he'd left his phone on his nightstand and had it set to vibrate. The sound was enough to wake him up even from a deep sleep.

He was dressed quickly and in his car before he knew it. It was a long drive across Vinton and then all the way to the Inn, but it was worth it. He didn't need to get a paycheck to drive that far for the woman he'd fallen in love with. It was a new feeling and he treasured it.

The sudden devotion he felt for her was odd, but he was flattered that she had texted him. Whether he was first on her list didn't even matter. That she had reached out to him did.

He was awed by how quiet everything was as he drove. His Toyota hummed quietly as he jetted down the highway, doing nine over the speed limit. It didn't really matter. He was the only one on the road. It was after the bars had closed and the drunks had made their way home. The only thing he saw besides the darkness and a few stray cars were big eighteen-wheelers. He liked the ones with the strings of lights around the cabs and trailers the most.

He couldn't see the Inn in the distance, even when he was close enough. Everything was dark until he crossed over the top of a hill and began the descent toward the Inn. The long, winding two-lane road was fun to drive when there wasn't anyone else in his way.

The lights of the parking lot at the Inn lit up the sky above the entire building. Eddie looked at it, wondering what Molly was doing now. He tried to picture her and realized that he would finally see her suite. He would see where she lived and how she lived. It was the lap of luxury so he'd heard.

He was about to park close to the Inn in the parking lot when he decided he didn't have to obey regular traffic laws. He was on private property and was certain Steven wouldn't have him towed if he parked alongside the curb in front of the long, wide structure.

He glanced up at it as he hopped out of the car. It had a majestic front, that was for sure. High arches along the outside, peaks and valleys, upside down teardrop windows, and only the fanciest and prettiest flower bushes placed purely for aesthetics along the front and throughout the parking lot.

Eddie was glad the front door was even open. The receptionist behind the desk looked up at him when he entered and then back down at the desk he was sitting in front of. Eddie assumed the man was reading.

He passed quickly and went down the short, wide hallway where the elevators were.

He hit the button and waited patiently for them to open.

The moment they did, he realized something.

He didn't know which suite was hers. He glanced back at the receptionist, but instead of asking what room she was in, he pulled his phone from his pocket.

I'm here, he texted her, *but I don't know which suite is yours. I'm in the lobby.*

He didn't have to wait long. The three dots came up and waved for only a moment before the number popped up.

210

The doors were about to close when Eddie shoved his hand between them and stopped them. He got on the elevator and pushed the button for floor two.

As he went up to the second floor, which took only a few seconds, Eddie reviewed the darkness he'd seen when he arrived. He'd looked down toward the water as he made his way around the curving road that went to the Inn, but he'd seen no light.

It had been nearly an hour since she'd texted him. Anything could have happened in that amount of time. But he was sure if she'd been afraid, she would have let him know.

He stepped off the elevator and looked at the plaque on the wall. It said rooms 201 through 205 were to the right and 206 through 210 were on the left. He moved his eyes directly to the left and her door was right in front of him.

Smiling, he crossed to it. He hadn't even lifted his hand when it was abruptly pulled open. Molly reached out and grabbed his arm, yanking him inside. He almost stumbled, but managed to stay on his feet.

"Whoa!" he exclaimed. "Are you all right?"

"I'm glad you're here," Molly replied, an urgency in her voice that he would have thought would have lessened in the amount of time it took for him to get there. "I tried to get Steven up, but he is either very asleep or not in his suite."

Eddie was surprised to hear that. Steven seemed like the most reliable man on the planet.

He gritted his teeth and widened his eyes. "You don't think something happened to him, do you?"

Molly gave Eddie a fearful look. "I think some sleeping pills happened to him. It's not like he has to be on constant guard. I don't want him to think I'm a baby either. Or paranoid."

Eddie nodded. "Okay, well, did you stop to think it might be him down there at the boatyard?"

Emily shook her head. "I don't think it's him. I think he would warn us if he was going down there at night.

"So you didn't call Steven or the police then?"

Molly shook her head. "No. I don't want to be a bother. Nothing has happened so far. I'll check the cameras tomorrow. And text Jack first thing to tell him to be on the lookout. That man might have been planting a bomb."

Eddie didn't think that was really likely. There had been no bomb threats. If this was all Vinnie's doing—and it was already established that he was the one skulking around the boatyard looking for the treasure—he wasn't there to bomb anything. He was there to dig. And digging was something a person could do quietly. All he'd need was a light and a shovel.

Molly pulled away from him, holding her phone in front of her between them. "I want you to see something. Look at this text I got."

She turned the phone around, and he took it from her.

"Good Lord," he said. "He's threatening to kill you now?"

Molly nodded, pulling the phone back toward herself. "And he said next, which means he's already killed someone. At least that's the way I take it."

Steven's face swam through Eddie's mind, and his heart wrenched in his chest. "Then we need to find Steven now!" he exclaimed. "He might be in big trouble."

Molly caught Eddie's arm as he was about to turn to the door. His body was tense with fear for his boss, but Molly didn't look worried.

"No. He hasn't gotten to Steven. I don't think he'd be that brave. I think he means Teresa. I think she's the one he's killed."

Sadness filled Eddie. He frowned and tilted his head to the side. "Oh no. You're probably right. How awful for her. What does she have to do with any of this, anyway?"

"I don't know. Maybe he thought she was a friend of Steven's or one of our group. Vinnie doesn't know anything about the Inn or any of us. No more than anyone else would know. He's never worked for Steven and none of us know who he is. Paula took the kitchen sabotage in stride and that's a good thing. She's going to have another baby with her husband and they don't need this kind of threat going on in their lives right now. Same thing with Dani. Steven's wife is going to have those twins, and she doesn't need to be bothered by any of this."

"Well, I guess it's a good thing neither are getting involved then."

"I don't even know if they really know what's going on."

"Dani was at the dinner the other night. She knows. But you're right. She is wise to stay out of it."

Molly began to pace back and forth in front of the couch. Eddie moved to sit down, his legs suddenly weary. His whole body was tired. He was going to pay for this in the morning.

But he didn't care. He was with Molly, and that was all that mattered.

He glanced around him, surprised that there was no TV or any kind of electronics in the place.

"You must not spend much time here," he said.

Molly gave him a confused look. "What do you mean? Why wouldn't I?"

"Well there's no TV or anything. No entertainment."

She let out a soft laugh through her nose and took a remote from beside the couch. She aimed it at the wall and pressed a button.

To Eddie's utter astonishment, the wall separated and a huge TV emerged from where it had been hidden. All around it were game systems. A DVD player, even a VCR player. There were a few boxes and gadgets he didn't recognize.

"Well, I'll be," he murmured, highly impressed.

Chapter Twenty-Three

Molly turned away from the TV. She resumed her pacing, still clutching her phone in one hand and the remote in the other.

"I want to go down there and explore right now," she murmured, "but I don't know if he's gone yet." She gave him a sharp look. "You look," she demanded.

Eddie stood up, sweeping his eyes around the room. "Where? What do you want me to do?"

"Look out the window," Molly directed, leading him to the door of her bedroom. When she was halfway across her bedroom, she turned to see he hadn't followed her. He was staring into the room as if it was out of bounds and he was in elementary school.

"What are you doing?" she asked. "You can come in here. I wouldn't have come in here if you couldn't, too. Weirdo."

He let out a soft chuckle and entered the room, still looking a bit hesitant. Molly thought that was probably the sweetest thing in the world. She never would have expected a man to do something like that. Not in the 21st century. Maybe in the romance novels she used to read.

She waved him over to the double glass doors. She had tied the billowing curtains to the side, but both were still moving softly in the breeze. "I saw the light out there. Look. It's gone now. But you can see along the shoreline because of the moon. It's full tonight."

"The moon is full," Eddie remarked, coming to stand next to her, his eyes directed at the boatyard in the distance. "Maybe what you saw was a werewolf."

She didn't know how he expected her to answer, but she chose to take the ball and run with it.

"That could be," she said seriously. "But I heard no howling or growling. Plus, werewolves aren't known for this part of Virginia."

Eddie snickered, a delightful little sound that made her look at him. His face was somewhat round, but his features fit him well. His eyes were bright when they looked at her. She felt like he was looking into her soul and moved her gaze away from him. He was a handsome man, she thought, and he probably didn't even know it. He certainly didn't carry himself like he did. So he would never be an action star. She didn't care about that.

She narrowed her eyes, putting her gaze back on him. "It's not you, is it? You aren't the werewolf, are you?"

Eddie shook his head vigorously, lifting both hands. "No, ma'am," he replied. "No fangs or hairy backs in my family."

Molly was relieved by his sense of humor. It made her feel much less tense. She crossed her arms and focused on the shoreline down by the piers where Steven and Jack had been digging. "He was near the piers. Where Steven thinks the treasure is. He must be getting close, too."

"For all we know, he found it tonight," Eddie said.

Molly pressed her lips together, giving him a sarcastic look. "I think I would have heard some kind of whooping and hollering if that had been the case."

"Not if he didn't want to get caught, you wouldn't have," was Eddie's on-point response.

"Well, I want to go down there. You don't see anyone moving around, do you?"

Eddie leaned further toward the balcony. He put his hand on the knob and glanced at her for what she assumed was her permission.

She lifted one hand, gesturing toward the door while nodding.

He turned the knob and stepped out. Molly felt a cool breeze brush past her.

She followed him out and they both leaned on the railing with both hands, staring down at the boatyard. Molly felt the breeze lifting her dark hair from her shoulders. It was a pleasant feeling. She had made sure to take it out of the bun she slept in and gave it a good brushing before Eddie got there. No sense in letting him know this soon what her bedtime ritual was. Her hair was long. She couldn't just let it fall free all night long as she tossed and turned. She'd wake up with mop head every morning and feel like shaving it all off.

"I don't think there's anyone down there," Eddie said quietly. He looked at her. She returned his gaze, feeling a tingle of attraction slide through her. "Do you?"

She shook her head. "No. You want to go down there?"

"Yeah." She was happy he was willing to go with her. There was no way she would have gone by herself. "Let's go see what we can find, shall we?"

Molly hurried to the living room to get her shoes on. She'd pulled on some socks just in case he was willing to investigate with her, but didn't walk around her suite with shoes on if she could help it.

The two went down in the elevator side by side, armed with their phones at the ready for flashlights or 911. Molly was aware that he was standing so close she could feel the brush of his fingers against hers and his sleeve against her arm. She wanted to grab him and imagined what his response would be if she laid a big kiss on him right there in the elevator. Would he pull away from her? Would she look like an idiot?

These thoughts kept her from acting on what she wanted to do. They were off the elevator quickly. The receptionist, Alfred Tennyson Lancaster, as he proudly announced to everyone who would listen, looked up at them and then back down at whatever he was reading.

Molly could resist it no longer once they were outside. They had held hands before, she told herself. He'd grabbed her hand just the same as she'd grabbed his. So maybe now it wouldn't be too inappropriate to walk down the boatyard hand in hand. She was afraid he would think it was childish.

Once she was outside, she couldn't help it. It was extremely dark, as the lights from the parking lot were on the other side of the building. The light was reflected off the sky and the moon was full and bright, but it was still uncomfortably dark, especially the closer they got to the water. The trees were casting long shadows, and the breeze made them move in strange, frightening ways.

Molly kept her senses about her, though. She wasn't one to frighten easily but then, how would she know really? What kind of situations had she ever been in that would test her bravery?

This was the only one. She didn't want to look weak in front of Eddie, but at the same time, she wanted his reassurance, his protection, his strength.

She grabbed his hand and hurried down the winding sidewalk, her phone light directed at the ground so she could see where she was going.

Eddie didn't pull his hand away. Nor did he say anything. He just held her hand all the way down the hill and didn't let go, even when they'd reached their destination. It was Molly who had to let go first. She decided it was a good sign. It meant he wanted to hold her hand as much as she wanted to hold his.

With a profound sense of satisfaction and glee, Molly changed hands with her phone and headed toward a spot on the ground that looked newly unearthed.

Chapter Twenty-Four

Eddie dutifully followed Molly as she moved with confidence past the places where her friends had been digging, looking for the treasure.

"You know what's strange," Molly said as she went.

"No," he replied in a quiet voice. "What's strange?"

Molly glanced at him. Her face was in shadows, but he still thought she looked beautiful. The moonlight only flattered her appearance even more. "That Steven and Jack are sure the treasure they are looking for is around these piers. He's told me several times that he's sure it's here, they're just missing it. And every time we've spotted Vinnie around here, he's been up that way. Not so close to the piers. But then tonight he comes back and he's closer to the piers."

Eddie followed along with her narrative, but wasn't sure what point she was trying to make.

"What do you take from that?" he asked.

She pointed the light on her phone at the replaced dirt near the beginning of the trees in front of them. Eddie could tell that was where they were headed. That's where she believed Vinnie had been that very night. That meant that if he was anywhere still around or if he returned, he would find them there.

What if he had a gun?

Eddie wished he carried one on him. He had no defense if Vinnie was carrying one.

It was hard to imagine the man he'd talked to in the café being so dangerous, though. He could still see Vinnie's charming smile and hear his laughter when he told them jokes or responded to one of theirs. He had caught Emily's attention. She'd seemed to like him when they were talking.

He just hadn't seemed that dangerous to Eddie. Suspicious, yes. Dangerous, not so much.

Eddie stopped a few feet away from the replaced ground when Molly reached it first. She got on her knees and plunged one hand directly down into the dirt. He blinked rapidly, unable to believe she could be so brave. What if there was something dangerous under there? Like a snake? Or something that could bite her and end her life tragically early?

He was about to tell her to be more careful but stopped when he saw she was using her hand like a shovel, flipping the dirt out of the refilled hole so quickly, it would have been amazing to see anything grab hold of her hand long enough to bite her.

Eddie regretted his unfortunate decision not to say something when Molly cried out in pain and yanked her hand back toward her chest. She instinctively dropped her phone into the dirt and instantly vanished into the shadows.

Eddie turned his phone directly on her. She was clutching her scooping hand to herself. When his light beamed on her, she looked to the side and snatched her own phone back up. The light was still on and beaming bright.

"You okay?" Eddie asked, concerned for her.

"I hit something hard," Molly replied, a slightly triumphant tone to her voice. "Nearly broke my fingers. But I didn't. Probably just jammed them or something."

"You should go to the doctor," Eddie advised. "Make sure none of them are broken."

She shook her head and Eddie didn't say anything more. It was not his business to tell her what to do, and he knew it. "No, I can wiggle them, see?" She made a fist and wiggled them all for him. It was brave of her, since Eddie could see the tremendous pain it caused her to do those things.

"Well, please just promise me you'll stop digging like that. And stay out of boxing matches for the next six weeks."

It was almost like she didn't understand he was joking at first and then half her lips lifted in a cocky grin. "I'll do both of those if you get over here and dig with me."

Eddie rolled his eyes. "If I gotta." He trudged to where she was but dropped his façade when he got there, going down to his knees and directing the light on his own phone down into the hole she'd made.

"I don't see anything other than this big rock right here." He pressed one finger against it to make sure it was a rock. It was large and oval. It could have been a dinosaur egg. Or an ostrich egg.

But it was a rock.

"Let me see," Molly said, getting closer to the object. She directed her light on it and stared for a good, long time. Eddie didn't know what to expect. It was like she was in a trance or just thinking deeply to herself. "I think this is the same rock we saw him taking out of here," she mumbled.

He didn't say anything, pressing his lips together. Vinnie had removed a large rock and then put the large rock back?

"I don't understand," Molly said, voicing his thoughts. "Why would he do this? Why would he take a big rock from this land and then return it? I don't understand."

"I think I know," Eddie replied, an idea springing to his mind. "You remember that movie where the guy wants a treasure, but it's on a weight so he has to replace it with something of equal weight so the traps don't kill him?"

Molly raised her eyebrows. "Indiana Jones?"

"Yeah, that's it. Well, maybe he took the rock so that when he found the treasure, he could replace it with the rock."

Molly frowned. Eddie knew the idea was ridiculous. He just couldn't think of any other reason why Vinnie would do what he did.

"Or maybe this isn't the same rock," Molly suggested. "Maybe this is another large oval-shaped rock, and he was so frustrated with having found a second one, he left it here. It's obviously not a treasure. Unless it's got gold underneath a layer of black."

Eddie thought her theory was probably as off as his was. He leaned in and pushed his hand into the dirt around the rock until he felt the other side. It was an oval, for sure. Once his hand was on the other side, he jiggled it to see if it would move. It did and easily.

"I think he put this rock here. I think he replaced whatever he took out with this rock." He sat back on his haunches, directing his light toward her feet, but his eyes were on hers. "I'm afraid to say I think he found the treasure. Which actually might be a good thing. If he's threatening you, you will be safe now. He's got what he wants. And Steven doesn't have to worry about the state of the Inn, right? He's got lots of money."

"Not as much as people think," Molly replied quietly. "He sunk a lot of his personal wealth into this place to make it nice again. He might live a nice life but he doesn't have the money he once had."

"I didn't know that," Eddie said in a regretful tone.

Molly gave him an affectionate look. "Don't feel sorry for him. He's still swimming in it."

They both laughed.

"So, what do you want to do now?" Eddie asked. "Are you sure this is where you saw the light?"

Molly stood up and looked around them. He got to his feet, as well, and did the same thing. There were other places where the earth had been disturbed and then put back, but Molly didn't seem concerned about any of them.

"I guess we'll head back to bed, then," Molly replied. "We'll look at the video footage in the morning. I have to make sure I erase this so people don't see me on camera." She directed her light toward him, grinning. "I look like a beached whale on camera."

Eddie snorted loudly. "Yeah, I don't think so," he stated firmly. Molly couldn't have been more than a hundred and forty pounds and almost his height, which was five foot six. She was probably five foot five. He wasn't a great judge of weight, but he knew when someone was obese and Molly was far from it.

"Come on." He held out his hand and felt a measure of relief when she took it. "I'll walk you to your rooms."

"You can stay on my couch," Molly said quickly. "I don't want you thinking you have to drive forty-five minutes home. Unless Jackson Jr. needs you in the morning."

Eddie was overwhelmed by a sudden urge to kiss her. She had remembered about his bird best friend. He squeezed her hand and smiled. "I'll text my neighbor to go over and take care of him. We've been neighbors and friends since I bought the place. She'll do it for me."

Molly blinked at him, keeping his gaze on her. "She?" She asked the question in the tone of voice one might expect from a jealous wife.

He grinned. "Yes, Molly. She. *She* is my very dear seventy-year-old, very much like a grandmother neighbor. And she will take care of Jackson for me."

They laughed together as they went up the curving sidewalk back to the Inn.

Chapter Twenty-Five

Molly stared at the monitor. She'd brought Steven and Jack in with her to the VT room so they could review the footage from the night before with her. Eddie would join her as soon as he was ready. He'd had some actual business to take care of that couldn't wait. A deadline for a major advertisement company bid or something like that. She didn't know the details. That was his expertise, not hers.

"There." She stabbed the monitor with her finger, glad that it was a different hand than the one she'd used the night before when she'd rammed her fingers into the rock. "You see him?" She tapped the screen, pausing it with the click of a button. She swirled around to look up at Steven, who was behind her to the left. His arms were folded over his broad chest and his eyes were narrow.

"I see him," he replied. His eyes rolled to her. "I'm going to start having some really sleepless night because of you, girl." He leaned forward, planting his hands on the table, his eyes moving back to the monitor. "So he's there again. But what's he doing? You would have come and got me if you found out he was doing anything bad. Right?"

"Of course," Molly was regretful but tried to keep the sound of it out of her voice. "Eddie and I went out there and checked and he was... just digging holes... I guess like you and Jack. But there was something strange about it and I..." Molly stopped talking, letting her words trail off as she watched what Vinnie was doing.

To think she'd been up in her rooms, aware of his presence, knowing he was up to something and was now watching everything she couldn't see... it was almost overwhelming. "He's digging and digging. I wonder if he knew how deep he wanted to go?" She mumbled the question mostly to herself, and neither of the men answered. She glanced up and over her shoulder to see they were both still watching the video. Although their eyes darted to her for a second, in the next one, all three had their eyes back on the screen.

"He's digging even further." Molly was confused. He seemed to be going down past where she and Eddie had found the rock.

The door behind them opened, shedding light into the dark room. All three turned and waved their hands at Eddie, shushing him while waving him in. He approached, and Molly stared once more at the screen. Chills covered her entire body when she saw Vinnie take something from a black bag behind him. He lowered the object into the ground.

"That's not the rock we saw," Eddie stated plainly.

Molly's eyes widened as fear penetrated her every nerve. She jerked around and stared at Steven. His eyes met hers.

"He buried something," Steven said in a deadly voice. "*He buried something*!"

The next moment, Steven was out the entry door with Jack and Eddie close behind him. Molly's breath had caught in her throat. She turned back and rewound the video to the moment Vinnie pulled the object from his bag. She tried to zoom in but couldn't make out what it was.

"What did you bury, Vinnie?" she whispered, terrified. "What did you bury?"

She couldn't move as quickly as the others. She didn't know what she was getting into. They were men, brave and tough and strong. She chose to be the weaker sex in this instance.

Eddie popped his head back in, breathless from running.

"Steven says get your butt out here," he said.

Molly let out a humorless laugh, looking at the screen one more time before getting up from the chair and reluctantly following Eddie out the door.

"I don't know why he wants me out here," she said as she and Eddie hurried to the elevator to go to the bottom floor. "I don't know anything."

"He's calling the cops now. He thinks it might be that bomb we kept talking about at the beginning. But I don't think it is."

Molly stared at him. They'd reached the elevator. "What do you think it is?" she asked.

Eddie pressed the button. He was tapping one foot anxiously, adding to Molly's nervousness. The doors slid open, and he held out a hand to her so she could pass in front of him and get on first.

"I don't know what it is," he replied. "I just don't think it's a bomb."

He looked around them as the door closed. She wondered why.

"I... I just have a feeling," he said, his voice quiet. "I saw that box on the screen and... well, I have really good... intuition. Sometimes I think it's... well, it sounds silly but a bit psychic. Like premonitions and things like that."

"Oh, really?" Molly was fascinated by the subject. She had no idea if such things were real and possible, but chose not to doubt people who said they had "feelings" about things.

"Yeah. And when we were digging like that last night and hit that rock... I wonder why he would put a rock like that on top. And I still say he's not trying to blow anything up. He wants the treasure. He wouldn't blow it up so no one would have it. He wants it for himself. He's going to do things quietly."

Eddie shrugged. Molly was impressed with his analytical thinking.

"I see where you're coming from," she said.

"Good. I can barely see that myself." She chuckled with him and he continued, "I just think that after meeting him and really talking face to face with him, if he's after the treasure, that's what he's here for. Not to hurt anyone."

"Oh!" Molly had a sudden thought. In all the excitement, she'd forgotten to tell Eddie what she'd discovered from the email address sending her text messages. She whipped her phone from her pocket and held it out to him. "Look at this," she said. "I want you to look at this and tell me what you see."

She put it a little close to his face, and he backed off, taking the phone from her hands.

"I saw this," he said with a frown. "What am I looking for? Some kind of code?"

"No, look." Molly reached over and manipulated the text message until he could see the email address of the sender. "It's not attached to a cell phone. At least this message isn't. Maybe the others were, but this one was mistakenly sent on an email account. Look at that address." She read it aloud. "1SA.B.LABLLC. The one might represent the father."

The doors opened, and three people tried to enter without letting the two of them off. They were on the ground floor, so when the people saw them, they backed off and let them step out. This distraction was only momentary, and when they were away from the doors and on their way down to the boatyard, she continued. "Not the Father, like God, but the father in this case, which is Sabatino. Then we have Sa and a b, that can easily be Sabatino and then we have lab. LaBrock! You see? LLC is nothing. That's a corporation tag. There's nothing about this address that doesn't scream Sabatino LaBrock. You have to admit it."

Molly's excitement made her voice raise in octave and volume. She became aware of it, and looked around urgently. No one was watching them, but she had the creeping feeling that Vinnie was somewhere nearby, watching everything they did.

She turned her upper body, scanning their surroundings.

"I hope he isn't watching us right now," she breathed.

Chapter Twenty-Six

The boatyard was practically deserted when they got down there. Typically, during the day, it was bustling with action as people rented out canoes, boats, jet-skis, and other water equipment. People also frequented the shop before they took out their own boats from the storage yard.

Steven had sent everyone away, apparently. Molly really thought that was for the best.

She was aware that Eddie was right beside her as the two went past the piers to the place just beyond where a group of men were standing. Steven and Jack were among those men. They were talking in serious tones. Several other men were wandering around, looking at the trees, the ground, the boats, as if they were secret service checking for snipers or other dangers.

She wondered who they were.

Steven caught sight of her and broke away from the men, coming down the slope quickly. "Molly," he said. "I've got bomb people on the way."

"Bomb people," Molly repeated. She would have been amused if it hadn't been so serious.

"Yeah. They're bringing a dog. If the dog doesn't sniff out a bomb, we're allowed to dig it up. If it does, we can't. They have to."

Molly raised one eyebrow, glancing at Eddie. "That's silly," she said. "Eddie and I dug it up last night and then replaced the dirt. I got it out with my hands. It's soft. There's a big rock down there. It's probably on top of whatever he buried, but that rock is there first. You can dig down to it."

Steven nodded. "That's true." He turned to the group of men standing around the refilled hole. "Get the dirt out down to the big rock," he called out. "Molly did it with her hands. You should be safe. But don't go past the rock. Maybe that will make it easier for the dog." He turned back to her. "They should be here in about ten minutes. Don't go anywhere."

"I wouldn't miss this for the world," she murmured. She tapped on Eddie's chest with the back of her knuckles. "Come on. Let's see if anything's changed since we put the dirt back in there."

He looked confused. "What do you mean? What could have changed?"

"That's a good question," she responded. "If anything has, we'll know and can tell them."

He didn't say anything else. She jiggled his arm, and he followed her over to where they were pulling the dirt out of the hole again, this time with shovels.

"It's not very deep to the rock," she said, with a note of caution in her voice. "You don't want to slam that shovel down in there too hard, do you?"

She didn't think it was a bomb, either. Not after listening to Eddie's wise words. She pondered whether he should tell them to Steven, who was a reasonable man. She looked at him, studying his oval face from the side. Her heart did a little jump when he turned his eyes to her and gave her a smile.

"Go tell Steven what you told me. About why you don't think it's a bomb."

Eddie glanced at Steven, doubt on his face. "I will, but I don't think that's going to keep him from going about this in the safest manner possible. Even if I'm right, wouldn't it be better to err on the side of caution? I mean, the bomb squad is already on its way. They've got the dog, like he said."

"True, true," Molly said with a nod. "I guess it is better to just wait and see if we... I mean, you are right."

He grinned at her. "Probably so..." he remarked.

The bomb squad was there quicker than Molly had expected. Coming from the main road, it only took a minute or so to get to the boatyard. They were on scene, letting a long, slender dog out of the back of the SUV only moments later. Molly watched with a smile when the dog immediately put his nose to the ground. She could hear the affectionate tone of the trainer, saying gently, "Where is it? Where is it? Is it here? Where is it, boy? Go find it."

The dog's tail wagged like mad as it ran from one place to the next, sniffing. He stopped at all the large holes, examining them closely, sniffing them, pawing at the dirt, before running off to another one. He came to the hole where the unearthed dirt exposed the rock.

The dog was very interested in the rock. His handler came over to where they were and gestured for everyone around the hole to move back. The dog sniffed a little longer than usual at the rock. Or what Molly thought was longer than at the other holes.

Still, he lifted his head out of the hole and continued to run around, sniffing holes and finding nothing.

"No bomb here!" the handler called out, lifting one arm. "All safe. All safe."

Molly heard the collective sigh lift up from the men around her. She let out one herself, even though Eddie had convinced her it wasn't one in the first place.

Eddie was already on his knees at the hole, pulling on the rock. Molly was glad because it had been much too heavy for her to move the night before. He was joined by Jack and with the both of them, the rock was dislodged and soon came up as easily as if it weighed an ounce or two.

"It must have been caught under a jutting rock or something," Eddie said. "It's not that heavy at all."

"Vinnie carried it," Molly said in a reasonable voice.

Eddie nodded at her. "Exactly."

"So, what do we have here?" Jack asked, reaching back into the hole. He leaned in quite far, Molly thought, and stood watching anxiously. She noticed when the bomb squad members and all the other men who had come to help stayed to see what it was, too.

They were now all holding their breaths for a different reason.

Jack rose up out of the hole, holding a square metal box. It was latched shut, but not locked.

"What is that?" one of the men in the crowd murmured.

"It's a box, moron," another said, jostling the first with his elbow.

"Shut up," the first one snapped. "I know that. What's in it, is what I'm wondering."

Both men stared at the box again. Molly wondered if they were brothers.

"Open it, Jack," Steven said. "Maybe it's the treasure."

"He's not gonna rebury the treasure he's looking for," Jack remarked, flipping the small latch and turning the lid over to expose the contents.

"What's in the box?" one of the men called out. Others in the crowd gave him amused looks.

"It's an ID and a bunch of other stuff," Jack replied. He pulled out a card. He stared at it. "Teresa Knox," he read.

"What?" Molly felt like someone had punched all the air out of her lungs. She felt her knees giving out. The next moment, she found herself holding onto Eddie, who had caught her before she hit the ground. "No," she said quietly, her coworker's worried face flashing before her eyes. "She... she was the first. Eddie... she was the first..."

"No," Eddie murmured into her ear. She shut her tear-filled eyes and listened to the sound of his voice. "No, no, Molly. These are just her things. That doesn't mean she's dead. It doesn't mean he's going to... to..."

"He's going to kill me," Molly sobbed. "He's going to try to kill me if he doesn't find that treasure." She turned her head to face Steven without letting go of Eddie's strong arms around her. "Steven, you have to find it. Whatever it is, you've got to find it, so he will stop this!"

Steven's face was like stone. His jaw was set. Molly had never seen him look as angry as he did at that moment.

"No," he replied, bluntly. "We have to find *him*. And we *will* find him. I give you my word."

Chapter Twenty-Seven

Eddie's heart ached for Molly. He didn't want to leave her side. She took the box of Teresa's things from Jack and went through them, crying the whole time. No one could make her stop except the police, who told her they had to take the box and its contents as evidence.

"Molly, let me make you a nice dinner," he suggested, leading her up the concrete sidewalk to the Inn. "I think you need to take some time off. I mean just today, that's all. Or longer if you want to. It's up to you. Whatever you want to do."

He wanted to be accommodating, but his overzealousness only succeeded in making her laugh.

"Oh, Eddie," she said, sucking in her tears, wiping them away with a surprising gesture of aggressiveness. "I would love to take the day off and have a nice dinner with you. You're really going to make it for me, though? Should I be scared?"

He grinned. "Not at all. Two years of culinary school under this belt. I can make something really special. How about we go to the store together and you tell me what you like? I'll make it for you, no problem. And you can meet Jackson! He's been asking about you."

"No, he hasn't!" Molly giggled at the idea, but Eddie was serious. He had talked about her to his friend enough to where the Molly Molly Little Dolly was going to get a nice surprise the first time she visited. He was glad to see her tears were ceasing. It was hard to watch her that way.

"He has. But don't worry. He's not the jealous type. He will welcome you. Mostly because he can't eat human food, so he has nothing to be jealous of. And he won't smell it. He's not a dog."

Eddie was proud of the fact that he seemed to be highly amusing to Molly. That was his goal, after all. He would distract her from this situation and the terrifying fact that Teresa's personal items had just been found buried in the ground by a terrorizing fortune hunter who might possibly be a murderer.

Eddie didn't want that thought to even enter his mind. His heart squeezed with fear when he thought of Molly being taken or murdered. And it looked like his assessment of Vinnie was wrong. He was the one on the video burying the box. The box contained items from the missing woman. The email address that sent the last threatening message had been too much like Sabatino LaBrock, a man who shared Vinnie's last name and had written a book about the Inn.

"Why did he bury it here?" Eddie asked. "That's what I don't understand."

"Maybe he was planning something," Molly replied. "What if he is trying to frame Steven? If he really does come after me next, he can make it seem like Steven did it. The evidence would be on Steven's property. He could say Steven was digging up those holes as a cover for the one that he buried Teresa's things in."

She stopped him when they were only a few feet from the doorway into the Inn. Her eyes were filled with tears. Eddie's instinct was to pull her into a hug, so that's what he did. He placed one of his hands on the back of her head and patted her soothingly.

"What if... what if she's here?" Molly asked in a frightened voice.

Eddie pushed her away enough so he could see her face. "What do you mean? Teresa? Here?"

Molly nodded, her wide eyes frantic. "What if he buried her here somewhere?" she whispered. She let out a sharp breath and pulled it back in again. "Oh, Eddie. I'm so frightened."

"I'm getting you away from here," Eddie stated firmly. He took her by the arm and hurried her through the door. "You just go on to your room and grab a bag. You can stay at my place. I have two extra bedrooms I don't use and a housekeeper who complains about never having a mess to clean up except for Jackson's mess." He tried to speak casually since Molly was already wound up as tight as she could be. "You wouldn't believe how much of a mess he can make."

Eddie couldn't quite tell what was going through Molly's mind, but she didn't disagree to come to his house. She went straight to the little hallway with the elevators. He stopped before the hallway, saying, "I'm going to talk to Steven, if I can find him. I'll tell him what's going on. I'm sure you've got vacation time you can take, don't you?"

"Yes, I do," Molly replied, nodding at him as she pressed the elevator button.

"Good. I don't." He let out a short laugh. "But I can work from home, no problem. I can show you what I do. I'll tell him you'll be there with me until this is resolved. Until Vinnie is caught and is behind bars. Okay?"

Molly nodded but said nothing. The desperate look on her face pulled on Eddie's heartstrings.

The elevator doors opened, and she stepped forward onto it, waving at him.

He waved back and waited until the doors had closed on the elevator before turning to head to Steven's office. Molly was in real danger. He had to get her out of there.

Steven agreed with him. Eddie's boss was in his office and the other men who had been out at the scene were crowded in there with him. Steven wasn't the only one who agreed Eddie should take Molly away from the Inn. Two detectives who seemed to be friendly with Steven and Molly and the Inn gang also expressed their concern and agreement.

A half an hour later, Eddie and Molly were leaving the Inn in his Toyota. The further they got from the place, the more Molly seemed to relax.

Eddie went a route that purposefully avoided the side of town where the café was. He didn't want to not be a part of the manhunt, but his place was certainly better served being at Molly's side, watching over her and protecting her.

"I'm going to keep you safe, Molly. I hope you know that." He couldn't help reaching out for her hand as he drove the highway. She squeezed his and smiled at him.

"I know, Eddie. I can tell. I'm glad to have you as a... friend." She said the word as if it wasn't what she meant. Eddie thought he might know why.

They were pulling into his driveway before he knew it.

"This is your house?" Molly asked, a bright look on her face. "I am impressed. Wow. Why on earth would you need a house so big?"

"I didn't have much space inside as a kid. It was me and a million other foster kids at the Lawlers. I loved those folks, really, but man, there were too many kids there. I felt like I couldn't turn around without running into some baby or other."

Molly laughed. His voice was so pleasant while he spoke. He didn't sound bitter, even though the words coming out of his mouth seemed so.

"So when I was offered this house, I couldn't resist it. It doesn't have a lot of rooms because the blocking walls have been removed. I like a lot of space. A *lot* of space."

"Well, I can't wait to meet Jackson," Molly said excitedly, sending a tingle through Eddie.

"Come on in, then. I'll get your suitcase."

Molly was out of the car and headed for his front door. Eddie moved as quickly as he could, getting her large suitcase from the back. She had a second smaller case that was probably her personal items, and he grabbed that as well.

He joined her on the porch and put his key in the doorknob. "Home sweet home," he said, glancing back at her. His words had more of an impact than he expected.

She blushed. His heart raced at the implication of the words.

"Yes," she said, softly. "And a very nice home it is."

Chapter Twenty-Eight

Molly was pleasantly surprised when she stepped into Eddie's home. She didn't know what she was really expecting... maybe she wasn't expecting anything in particular. But as soon as she entered, she knew it had to be the home of Eddie Button. The atmosphere seemed to fit him so well.

The walls were a soft white and the decorations he had around the room were bright and colorful. The curtains were a light blue color that reflected the sun into the living room and kitchen, creating a glow that made Emily feel warm inside.

She was immediately greeted by the fluttering of wings and a low rumbling sound. Her eyes settled on the large cage in the corner of the room. She could tell Jerry Jackson Jr. was a well fed, well-loved bird. She went straight for him, glancing over her shoulder at Eddie, whose grin was so boyish and cute, her heart melted right then and there.

"Hello," she cooed. "I'm Molly..."

She let out a little laugh when the bird said her name with her. Eddie hadn't been lying. He really had told Jackson Jr. about her.

"Molly. Molly." The bird repeated her name, walking back and forth on the perch in his cage. "Molly, Molly, Little Dolly. Friend. Friend."

Molly pressed her lips together, turning to Eddie, who had come up next to her. "Oh my, Eddie, what a bird! He's gorgeous *and* smart!"

"Jack is cute," Jackson Jr. chirped. "Jack is cute. Thank you. Thank you."

Molly put one hand over her heart. She couldn't help falling in love with the bird right then and there.

"All right, well, Jackson Jr. isn't getting all the attention today, okay, buddy? Molly is here to talk to me. So you just keep quiet over here. We're going to have talks. Me and her." He moved one finger between himself and Molly. She loved the gentle, reproaching voice he was using. "You hungry? Thirsty?"

"No. No." Jackson Jr. swayed his head from side to side. "No. No."

"All right. You be good and just look out the window at the neighborhood cats."

"Cats. Not food for cats. Not food for cats."

Molly giggled, moving away from the cage so the bird wouldn't think she was laughing at him. She walked into the kitchen, giggling even more because she was associating human traits with the bird because he talked like one.

"That's an amazing creature right there," she said in a low voice as Eddie followed her into the room. She sat at the table, feeling comfortable, as if she'd been there many times. "It must feel like you're living with another person sometimes."

Eddie glanced back at the cage, a look of affection on his face. "Sometimes, yeah. He's been a great companion for me since I brought him home. He wasn't a talker then. He was just a young bird."

Molly was surprised to hear that. Her eyebrows shot up, and she said, "So you taught him to speak like that?"

Eddie shrugged. "Yeah, I guess so. But I don't think I really had much to do with it. God just gave that bird a brain for learning and a voice box to use. He learned on his own just listening to me. He knows what words mean. Like when he called you Molly, Molly, Little Dolly the first time. He knows what all those words mean. You're the woman I met, Molly. He had a little fabric doll in his cage for a good while until it wore out. And he knows what 'little' means as opposed to 'big.' I didn't teach him that. He taught himself."

"Well, I think that's unbelievably cool," Molly replied, smiling widely.

"All right, shall we get our evening started with an appetizer?" Eddie asked, clapping his hands together in front of him and rubbing them gleefully together. It was a gesture Molly's father had often used when she was a child, and the similarity made Molly feel giddy for a moment. She'd had a wonderful set of parents who raised her in a functional home with a good life and having that memory of her late father pop up in her mind was almost like a sign. She was supposed to be there. Eddie was the man she had been waiting for.

An overwhelming feeling of nervousness made her drop her eyes to the table and pull in a deep breath.

Eddie was next to her a moment later, pulling out the chair next to her and sitting down. "You all right?" he asked, concern in his voice.

She looked up at him, nodding.

"You're not thinking about those messages or Vinnie, are you?" Eddie sounded irritated, but Molly didn't feel attacked. "I don't want you thinking about that stuff tonight. Not here in my house when we're having dinner. In fact, I'm hereby banning all talk about the crime, and the situation, and Steven, and all of that for this whole night."

Molly saw the humor in what he'd said. She hadn't been thinking about their situation at all. And she agreed that she didn't want it brought up.

"I can't promise I won't talk about Steven," she replied light-heartedly, "but I can definitely avoid all that other stuff. We can think of plenty of things to talk about besides that stuff. Like..." She looked around at his décor. "Like the beach, which you obviously like. Or... whales..." She lifted her eyes to a grand picture on the wall, a long rectangular depiction of a whale breaching water. It was a magnificent representation of the large mammal.

"You want to talk about whales?" Eddie sounded excited and his eyes sparkled at her.

She had to laugh. "Yeah," she replied with a nod, "let's talk about whales."

Chapter Twenty-Nine

Molly wasn't able to sleep that night when she returned from her evening with Eddie. He'd made her lasagna, and they'd watched a couple old episodes of Perry Mason. They hadn't really been watching, though. They were too involved in their conversation.

They'd talked about everything under the sun—everything except work. Neither mentioned the situation with Vinnie, or the treasure, or even Teresa Knox. As worried as she was, Molly knew Eddie was right. They both needed a night where they weren't thinking about it all.

Molly left that night and thought about him the entire way home. She was so comfortable with him. She liked being around him. She was fascinated by the way he'd grown up. From his perspective, he was alone because he was rarely given any attention. So he felt isolated even though there were so many people around, children his age, parents who treated him with kindness and loving authority.

He'd grown up well-rounded, but a true introvert because of that upbringing. His outlook on life was mostly positive, and he had no problem at all being alone. He liked his own company.

She'd thought about his bird friend. They'd hate a few more short conversations that evening. He was definitely the smartest bird Molly had ever seen. Then again, she'd never spoken to a talking parrot before. The bird might very well be normal as far as birds are concerned.

That night, she rolled over in bed and stared at her phone. Taking the night off of thinking about their problem, going so far as to keep her phone on silent and then forgetting she even had it because she was so involved in talking to Eddie.

Molly rolled over so that she was staring at the crack in the curtains, out at the night sky. There was light coming from somewhere. It couldn't be the parking lot lights because they were on the other side of the building. The only time light came through her window was when there was a boat coming into the dock.

She sat up in the bed, her eyes half-closed. She was tired—but not sleepy. She'd had such an exciting day. She should be exhausted and sleeping easy. Was something bothering her? Or was she just too elated about finally understanding why a woman might want to spend the rest of her life with a man? Truly and wholeheartedly.

If her brain was going to insist on being awake, Molly was going to find a reason to keep it occupied. If there was one thing she hated, it was when she wasted time lying in bed staring at the ceiling worrying about things that were completely out of her control. Those were the most annoying times.

Molly slid out of bed, reaching to her nightstand to grab her cell phone. She was tempted to text Eddie, but they'd just been together and she didn't want to look desperate. She thought about him, remembering his smile and the smooth way he talked. He had a delightful laugh. A contagious one that made Molly feel good inside.

She went to the window and pushed aside the light curtains, peering out into the darkness. There was a boat out there at the dock, with lights on and sound as people enjoyed a party on the deck. That was the light she was seeing.

Satisfied she didn't need to be afraid, Molly went to the writing desk near the other window. The curtains were a little thicker and darker, so no light came through that one.

Molly got a yogurt cup from the fridge and a spoon from the drawer before going to the writing desk and clicking on the lamp. She sat at the desk, putting the food and spoon to the side while she opened her laptop and typed in her password.

She opened the cup and took a mouthful of the yogurt while she was waiting for it to load up. She tapped the keyboard a couple times as it did so, shoveling the yogurt in her mouth like Eddie hadn't fed her a delicious, huge portion of homemade lasagna.

Once the laptop was ready for her, she clicked on the server that would take her to the security cameras of the Inn. She had access and put in the password so she could bring up the last five years' worth of video surveillance.

She typed in the dates she wanted and brought it up in a four-part sequence with four days playing at the same time.

Pausing the playback, Molly went into the kitchen to find something better to eat. Glancing at the clock on the stove, she was a little taken aback that it was 3:45 in the morning. She'd gotten five good hours of sleep, she thought, and that wasn't too bad. No wonder she was so awake.

She returned to the video after making herself a poached egg and some toast.

Molly settled in the chair, which was adorned with a black cushion underneath her and behind her. It was comfortable, but she was a bit chilly. She retrieved and robe and sat back down.

With a watchful eye, Molly found the dates and times when Steven's tires had been slashed—both times—and the fire had been set in Paula's kitchen. The fourth video was when Jack reported suspicious digging near the boatyard before they thought there might be treasure buried there. It had been dismissed as probably an animal.

The last thing Molly got with her for the session was a small container of powdered donuts. Set with a bottle of water, she sat at the desk and stared as the screen showed what had happened on those days.

It wasn't until then that Molly realized the person on the screen committing those acts of sabotage wasn't Vinnie. It couldn't have been Vinnie. On each occasion, the person committing the crimes was dressed head to toe in gray. A gray sweatsuit, gray shoes, and a gray hat on his head. Sunglasses covered his eyes. He was well covered, which was a good thing for him because the video was extremely clear. The only one that was grainy was the one showing the area around the dock. And on *that* video, it looked like Vinnie. A taller, lankier man than the person doing the previous sabotage. She'd seen Vinnie in person now. She knew those crimes hadn't been committed by him.

He might not have done those, but she was sure he had something to do with it. Somehow, they had to find that accomplice. That might lead them to the whereabouts of the elusive Teresa Knox, who may or may not be still alive.

Somehow, they had to find either Teresa or this accomplice. She had to show this information to Steven. It could wait but she didn't want it to wait. If she could have gotten away with taking the information to him at that moment and woken them all up with it, she would have.

Nothing could be done at that moment in time. A glance at the clock told her it had been an hour and a half, anyway. She could expect the world around her to start waking up at about six-thirty or so.

But it wasn't until she decided to turn on the tv and watch some early morning shows that her body decided it wasn't done sleeping. She'd pulled her comfy robe around her and sat down with the remote in her hand, only to find herself asleep and dreaming not long after.

She was lucky to wake up two hours later and get dressed quickly so she could make it to work and not be late. She felt like she'd been drugged. She had to get a big cup of coffee and drink it as she went down the elevator, her laptop under her arm, still left open to the video surveillance videos. They had been paused, and she'd taken several screen shots of the man on the screen. She hoped her friends would tell her she was seeing things and that the man was definitely Vinnie. The angle was just different, they'd say.

But she knew they wouldn't say that. Not even to humor her. The saboteur was a smaller man than Vinnie. There was no doubt of that.

Chapter Thirty

Eddie looked up abruptly, his heart jumping into his throat when the door was flung open. Molly came through with such a determined look on her face, his first thought was to wonder if he'd done something wrong. Should he be apologizing right now? He racked his brain for what they'd done the night before, going over everything he could think of that he'd said and done, searching for where he'd messed up.

"Wait till you see what I've found!" Molly blurted out, slapping her laptop down on his desk a little harder than she probably intended to. Fortunately, his thick calendar mat gave it some cushioning.

She leaned forward so far he thought she might be going in for a kiss. He was glad he didn't react to that because she immediately turned her face down, opening her laptop and pressing buttons on the front. She typed her password upside down and stood up straight, looking at his face.

He knew she expected some kind of reaction. He really wanted to give it to her, but when the pictures came up on the screen, he wasn't sure what he was looking at. It was obviously footage from the parking lot and alleyway CCTV cameras, and that same grainy video from the boatyard.

"Which one of these doesn't look like the other?" Eddie asked, keeping his eyes on the screen, determined to figure out why she was showing this to him. He was grateful when she circled around his desk and leaned down to look at the screen. She put her finger on the figure in each of the pictures.

"This... this... this... that's the person who committed the sabotage here before we discovered Vinnie's connection. That's a smaller man. You look at him and tell me that's Vinnie."

Eddie couldn't do it. He immediately knew the person on the camera footage wasn't the same man he met in the café.

He sat back, cupping his chin with his hand, splaying his fingers over his lips, his eyes still on the screen. She tapped a button and all the videos moved at once. Eddie's gaze flicked around the screen as he watched the videos play out. He wasn't happy about the sabotage to Steven's car. And watching the flames lick through the windows of the kitchen and the stream of people coming through the window looking frightened was almost too much for him.

He glanced at Molly, who wasn't watching the screen. Her eyes moved from side to side. He could tell she was thinking.

"Have you told Steven about this?" he asked.

She shook her head. "No. I think we should, though, tell him together, you know. I wanted to show it to you and see what you thought. You've gone through a lot of videos for social media, haven't you?"

Eddie thought about it.

"I guess I have," he replied, running through his memory. He'd taken several courses on recognizing fake or manipulated videos. He was constantly stunned by the level of technology and what was possible. He was adept at spotting manipulations, though, in both pictures and video. He'd never imagined he'd have a reason to use that skill in the professional workplace.

And it wasn't even for his real job there at the Inn.

"I don't know how that would be useful for us, though," he continued, watching the aftermath of the sabotage, as firemen and trucks pulled up to the alley where delivery drivers made their stops at the kitchen. He could see Paula in the background, hugging herself, a distraught look on her face. Steven had an arm around her shoulder before another man, whom Eddie assumed was Paula's husband, came over and took his place.

"If you watched these videos enough times, would you be able to spot anything about that second person that can give us any clues who they might be?"

Eddie felt put on the spot. On one hand, he was flattered the woman thought he was that skilled. On the other hand, he was fairly sure his talents weren't the level of Sherlock Holmes by any means.

"I'll take a few minutes to look through the videos a few times," he conceded, "but please don't expect much. I don't know what I'm looking for."

"Well..." Molly appeared to be thinking about it. Eddie couldn't help thinking about the night before when she'd been seated at his table, eating his lasagna and garlic bread, grinning and laughing when he told a silly joke, telling her own to share in his embarrassment. She'd been the best company he'd had in... forever... as far back as he could remember. He'd never had a better time with anyone else.

"I guess you want me to see if I think they've ever come here to the Inn. Not that I'd really know. I think that's more something Steven will have to look for. That's more along his lines, right?"

"Just watch them and see if you come to any conclusions."

Molly clearly had an agenda. She had something on her mind. He was ready to go along with it, if she would just tell him what she wanted him to look for. He wouldn't lie about it, but at least he'd know what it was.

"Okay."

She stayed where she was, her eyes on his face.

His eyebrows shot up. "Right now?"

"Yeah. Look through them right now while I'm gone. I'm gonna get Steven. I think he should see this, too. You're right. If there's something familiar about this person, he'd spot it first. He's really observant that way. Not that you aren't. Just that... like you said, he's been here a lot longer and all that."

Eddie was amused by the way she seemed to be defending herself when he was the one who thought Steven would be a better candidate in the first place.

She turned to the door, taking two steps toward it before stopping and turning on her heel. He'd been manipulating the mouse pad with the tip of his finger, his eyes on the screen, but when she turned so abruptly, she got his attention.

"I... I just wanted to say I had a really good time at your place last night, Eddie."

He could hear the gush of emotion in her voice. For only a moment, he was a little confused. Was that emotion really for him? It sounded like she was really attracted to him. It was such a new and different feeling. Like something had finally clicked into place. It was almost like his future, which had seemed certain, and not entirely bleak, was suddenly filled with fireworks and really bright colors. Kind of like the atmosphere he enjoyed in his house.

He shared her feelings and wasn't going to let her get out of his small office without telling her so.

To his own surprise, Eddie stood up and went around the desk, reaching out for her hand. She looked surprised but allowed him to take the one closest to him, which he held in both of his.

"I had a good time, too, Molly. I'd really like to do that again soon, if you want."

"You can't make me dinner though," she said. "I would rather make it for you. It's only fair."

He tilted his head to the side. "And you don't just do the microwave thing?"

Molly laughed, the pleasing sound making him feel tingly inside. "I can cook. I can follow a recipe. Just tell me what you want. What your favorite is. I'll make it. If it's not too complicated. I'm no French chef. We can get Paula to make dinner for us if you want some kind of foreign cuisine."

Eddie chuckled. "I think this is getting much too complicated. How about you make dinner next? But today, I have an idea for lunch. If you want to join me for it."

Molly nodded, much to his satisfaction, and hurried from the room without saying anything more than, "I'll be right back."

He sat behind his desk again and watched the CCTV footage, getting closer to the screen and watching the videos closely. The first thing he determined was that the footage from the boatyard *was* Vinnie.

The two occasions at Steven's car in the parking lot, and the one of Paula's kitchen were the same person, he deduced quickly. Molly was right, it wasn't Vinnie.

But Eddie questioned whether or not it might even be a woman, as opposed to a man.

And there was only one woman he knew of unaccounted for in this situation.

Teresa Knox.

Chapter Thirty-One

Molly was five feet from Steven's office when the cell phone in her hand buzzed. She looked down at it and saw a text had come in. With a slamming heart, she pulled down on the top bar menu to see who it was.

It was from Steven.

Come down to the pier, the last one after the shop. Wait till you see.

Molly grinned. He was such a big kid. She turned abruptly and went straight back to Eddie's office. She was still feeling overly warm from when he'd taken her hand in his. His eyes had spoken as much as the words from his mouth. He was falling for her. She was fine with that. She felt the same way.

The natural urge to be cautious was still there. But she was more inclined to trust him. Whether it was because she was attracted to him, or because he gave off a sense of trustworthiness naturally, she didn't know. Molly loved the feelings he gave her.

She turned the knob and stuck her head in. Eddie was just as she'd left him, his eyes on the screen of her laptop, his expression contemplative.

"Steven wants us down at the pier," she said quickly, jerking her head back. "He texted me anyway. You want to come along?"

Eddie was up and around his desk in a flash, which was amusing, and made Molly have to restrain a giggle.

"Don't have to ask me twice," he murmured. "Let's go see what's up."

They took the back hallway that led to the doors, letting out onto the hill with the long sidewalk down and around. It was really the quickest way if they didn't get a motorized vehicle.

"What's going on this time, you think?" he asked, hurrying next to her. Her heart had been beating normally until her eyes caught sight of what was down the hill from them.

Steven was pacing back and forth. She noticed he was quite near the spot where she had originally seen Vinnie snooping around. Jack was nearby, a shovel in one hand up and propped up on his shoulder. The other hand was placed firmly on his waist. She could see they were anxious just by the way they were standing.

"You think they found something?" Eddie's voice had suddenly dropped low. She glanced at him and met his eyes. The look that passed between them was almost heavenly. She felt a surge of warmth flood through her and had to look away.

"Maybe," she said breathlessly. She didn't feel that way at the thought of finding buried treasure. It was thinking of his touch and the way he looked at her that made her feel faint.

Molly was only a little surprised to see the door to the boat shop open onto the pier and three women came out. It was Paula and the wives of her friends. She quickened her pace, not wanting to hold everyone up by arriving late.

Eddie matched her pace without question.

"Well?" she called out loudly when she got close enough.

"We're waiting for you!" Steven yelled out, waving one hand. "I want everyone to be here when we pull this out."

"What if it isn't at all what he thinks it is?" she heard Eddie murmur behind her. "Isn't he afraid of looking... well, foolish, I guess?"

Molly shook her head. "No, probably not. When he means everyone, he means us. Not like he's called the Washington Post or anything."

Eddie laughed. "Right, I see."

They got to the others a few minutes later, and Jack immediately pulled the shovel from his shoulder. He looked at Steven with his eyebrows raised. "We ready for this?"

Steven nodded, a grin on his face. "We're ready. Let's get to digging."

Jack snorted, giving his friend the side-eye. "I like how 'we' are suddenly digging. You want the shovel?"

Steven's grin only widened. "You're so good at it, though, Jack. Come on, you know I can't get these hands all calloused up."

Jack let out a genuine laugh, stabbing the shovel into the ground.

Molly stopped a few feet away and watched. Eddie came up beside her, close enough to be touching her arm with his. In fact, he was a bit behind her, turned slightly sideways toward her. As if he might need to grab her and pull her away from something bad. Like a bomb.

She was impressed with the way he was always on his guard. Like he was somehow now her protector. It was another first for her.

Her eyes, along with all the others, were focused on the dirt Jack was pulling out of the ground. He'd already gone down about three feet. He was on his knees a few moments after she got there, pulling dirt out with his hands.

It was then that Jack's wife got to her knees and started helping him pull the dirt out. One by one, the rest of them did the same, including Molly and Eddie.

They all stared at the old box they'd uncovered. It was a metal trunk. The lock on the latch looked ancient. It required a huge key, probably made of brass or gold, whichever material the latch was made of. It was dark, faded, dirty, grimy... impossible to tell what metal it was made of.

"We have found the treasure," Jack said triumphantly, grinning at the rest of them. "Come on. Help me get this latch off."

They had all participated in pulling the large trunk out of the hole they'd dug. Before anyone else could respond to Jack's request, Eddie was on his feet and headed over to the shed behind the boat shop near the pier they were closest to. He yanked the door open and scanned the inside.

Molly watched him reach into the small shed and pull out a long crowbar.

"Perfect!" Jack said, reaching out for the crowbar long before Eddie was back for it. Molly was amused by how anxious her friend was to get the trunk open. She felt the same way. She was just hiding it better than Jack.

She was willing to bet, though, that Eddie could see how she felt if he wanted to. She couldn't help it. Their evening together had been the best time of her life. She wanted more nights like that. Longer nights. Ones where she could fall asleep in his arms and wake up to make him breakfast and coffee in the morning.

He was a gentleman. He was smart. He worked hard and made his own money. In her eyes, he was gorgeous and funny... very near to a perfect man.

"Ready?" Jack asked, slowly moving his eyes over his friends.

"Will you just do it, please?" Steven asked anxiously, his smile wide on his face.

Jack pushed the crowbar into the lock and pulled back hard. The lock snapped, shattering into several large pieces that fell to the ground with a soft clunk. Jack bent over and pushed the latch off the ring. He lifted the lid and slung it backwards so it hit the ground on the other side with a much louder clunk than the lock made.

Steven was the first one to actually reach into the trunk, which was fine with Molly and probably with the rest of them, too. This was his property, after all. Whatever was in the trunk belonged to him.

"Okay..." he said excitedly. "Let's see what this is."

He pulled out several long envelopes in terrible states of disintegration. The strings keeping the paper folders "closed" was really the only thing that seemed untouched by the years. The bits of twine looked like they might have been put there yesterday. Steven attempted to open the paper envelopes but they began falling apart in his hands.

He gently laid them back down and reached for the sacks next to the stacks of papers. He lifted one and "weighed" it with his hand. Glancing back at the rest of them, Steven stated, "Fairly heavy. Willing to bet either gold bars, coins or some kind of metal, maybe gems."

"Give me a bag. I want to look in one." Paula held out her hand.

With that, they all asked for one. Molly looked down into hers with an anxious heart.

"Gems." Paula's voice sounded amazed. She looked up at them with wide eyes, her bag open in front of her. "These gems will pay for my kitchen repairs and more, Steven. Can I have them?"

Steven grinned. "Of course you can. You each take a sack. I'll call the authorities and see if there's anything I need to do with this. It's my property, so I'm pretty sure it's mine, which means I have the right to distribute it among all of you. Merry Christmas early!"

They all laughed. Molly shared an astonished look with Eddie.

"I must be the luckiest guy in the world to stumble into this job," he mumbled.

The rest of them laughed even more.

Steven had just given them a fortune!

Chapter Thirty-Two

Molly stood on her balcony, amazed by how beautiful it was when the moon was nearly full. The sky was clear and the stars were glittering like diamonds in black velvet.

The boat drifting in the boatyard belonging to the party people had been in full swing until eleven o'clock sharp. Molly was almost impressed by how quickly it got quiet when the clock struck eleven.

She assumed that had to be the cutoff time by law and the people on the boat had probably been warned once or twice already.

Molly didn't mind the party people. She'd never seen or heard anything bad going on. There weren't any fights or shouting or signs of anger and aggressiveness. She heard a lot of laughter. She heard music that wasn't that bad to listen to. Some pop rock, some aggressive rock, with some R&B and some rap mixed in.

She wished she'd gotten the names of those people. As much as she thought about it, though, she couldn't justify going up to strangers and saying, "Hey, I've been watching you party from my window and thought I'd invite myself over to see what all the fun and laughter is about!"

No matter how tempting it was.

They would probably leave as soon as she got up her nerve, anyway.

Now, the waves slapped against the side of the boat, rocking it gently and Molly could picture what it was like inside there. She and her friends had taken boats out on short trips many times over the years. She was used to it now. Molly had great sea legs.

A breeze brushed over her shoulders, lifting her brown, wavy hair lightly. She felt the gentle wind blow down the back of her robe, making her pull it tightly around the front, a shiver running up her spine.

It wasn't a cold breeze. It was the sensation that made her shiver. It felt almost like a hand running down her back. She gripped the railing of her balcony and focused on the water below. She was on solid ground. The water wasn't close enough to affect her the way it would if she were on that boat.

Molly had nothing to fear.

She thought how amazing it was to know she was the owner of gems that were possibly worth millions of dollars.

Steven had given them away so freely. Granted, there were three bags of jewels left over that he took with him. He would always have the most. He owned the land. Certainly, none of them would complain about getting one bag. He didn't have to give them anything, and they knew that.

Molly heard a whisper behind her and turned around.

Or she thought she was going to turn around.

Suddenly, an arm snaked around her shoulders, and a hand wrapped around her mouth. The hand was holding a cloth. It stank and she struggled not to breathe it in. It wasn't possible! The words jolted through her mind as she felt her brain beginning to blur. It wasn't possible for someone in the twenty-first century to use a cloth covered in chloroform. How did people even get that stuff anymore?

It couldn't be. *It couldn't be.*

When Molly woke up, she was lying on a cold, hard floor. Her hands were bound in front of her. She could see them when she opened her eyes. For a moment, she wondered if they were really hers. Then she wiggled her fingers and knew... yes, they were hers. Those were her dirty, long fingers, the nails painted a festive pumpkin orange, just because she liked the way it looked against her skin. She lifted her head, realizing it was resting on concrete but not solid concrete. It was old, busted up in a lot of places, one of them being underneath her head.

It didn't matter, anyway. From the very moment she lifted her head to see around her, she felt such an intense spinning sensation, she had to close her eyes and let her head drop to the cold, hard floor once again.

She took in a deep breath. *Get it together, Molly*, she thought. *You will be missed. Someone will notice.*

But *when* would they notice? The morning? Five hours from now? Even one hour from now was an awful thought. She wanted to be rescued right then and there. She longed for Eddie, prayed for someone to try to find her for whatever reason. Long before any harm could come to her.

Her heart slammed in her chest as she lay on the cold concrete floor, praying harder than she'd ever prayed in her life.

"M... Molly?"

Her head snapped up, and she jerked so hard she realized her legs were bound at the ankle. There was a chain attached to her leg restraints that led to a pole two feet away.

Her eyes fell on a figure in the corner. It was shaded dark by a shadow, but Molly could tell by the voice that it was a woman. It only took another moment before she recognized the voice.

"T... Teresa?" she asked anxiously.

Teresa leaned forward, emerging from the shadow of the corner so Molly could see her.

Molly's heart began to race. The woman was dirty from head to toe. Her hair was matted on her head. Her clothes were as dirty as the rest of her, but they looked in good enough condition if Teresa had been taken the very day she'd left employment at the Inn. They weren't ripped or torn.

"I don't believe it!" Molly cried out softly. "It's you! I can't believe it! Have you been here this whole time? Did he hurt you? What has he done to you?"

Teresa's facial expression didn't change much. She gave Molly a forlorn look. "I've been here since the day after I left the Inn. I was hoping if I stayed with my cousin Heather, I'd be safe because I wasn't at home. I was wrong. He came after me there, too."

"But what does he want?"

The look on Teresa's face wasn't the most pleasant. Molly gave her the benefit of the doubt. She'd been holed up wherever they were for a long time now. Nearly a month.

"He wants that treasure, of course!" Teresa snapped. "I wish someone would just give it to him so he'd let me go. Us. Now us."

Molly didn't know if it was wise to play dumb. She just wanted to see how truthful Teresa might be under the current circumstances. If there was one thing Molly wasn't used to, it was keeping her mouth shut when needed. She liked others to know her opinion.

"There's no treasure," Molly said in a low voice. She was lying. She hadn't outright lied like that in a very, very long time.

She justified it in her mind by thinking that now there was no hidden treasure. Steven had found it. It was no longer hidden, and the treasure had been split up among the group.

"There is a treasure," Teresa said in a growling voice.

Molly stared at the woman. Terrible condition or not, something was... *off* about her.

Chapter Thirty-Three

Vinnie moved slowly. Molly wondered if the man knew she was aware of what he had been doing at the Inn. She was filled with questions, but her fear was pushing urgently at her. On one hand, she was comforted by the fact that Teresa was still alive. But even though only a short time had passed, Molly was becoming more and more suspicious of the woman.

She seemed too confident for a woman who had been held captive for a month.

Molly had read about Stockholm Syndrome, where a captive fell in love with or developed a devotion to their captor. Could that be what had happened here?

Vinnie went through the room as if he didn't see Molly there. She watched him, rolling her eyes as he walked from one side to the other. Teresa didn't say anything either. The strangest thing about that was that Teresa kept her gaze on Molly. Wouldn't she be looking at Vinnie too? Perhaps with a frightened look? It didn't look like she'd missed a month's worth of meals, that was for sure.

Molly was questioning this scenario more every second that passed.

"What do you want with me?" she asked courageously.

Vinnie spun around and stared at her. His eyes narrowed. Molly blinked at him. He looked astonished to see her.

The confusion she'd been feeling now almost overwhelmed her. Her eyes widened, and she looked from the man to Teresa and back again.

"What's going on?" she asked. "What... what are you doing taking me in the middle of the night like this?"

Vinnie seemed to compose himself quickly. He narrowed his eyes and curled his upper lip. "You just stay right where you're at, woman," he growled. "I've got plans and you aren't gonna ruin them."

"You have no right to keep us here, Vinnie!" Teresa yelled angrily.

Molly watched as Vinnie spun around again, as if surprised, and stared at Teresa. "You!" he cried out. Molly would have sworn she heard anger in his voice. But not the anger of a captor. It was the anger of someone betrayed. She would have sworn it.

"You've kept me down here long enough!" Teresa snapped, the same way she'd reacted to Molly's question. "You've got her now. You can let me go. I won't tell anyone. You can let me go and do whatever you want with her. She's friends with those people at the Inn more than I am. You can get more out of her!"

Vinnie appeared to be listening to the woman, his teeth grinding, his jaw visibly clenching and unclenching.

He stomped over to her and yanked her up to her feet. "You're coming with me," he growled. "We have some talking to do."

"No!" Teresa yelled. This time, Molly heard what she'd expected all along. Fear. "You can let me go now. You don't have to keep me! I won't tell a soul who you are or that you're here."

"You're right that I don't need you anymore," Vinnie replied in a smooth as silk tone. "You're not worth anything to me anymore. At all. And you really expect me to trust you not to say anything." He laughed.

Teresa's face had changed now. Molly could see her hands behind her back, working frantically at the rope loops that were there. They were stuck tight. There was no way she was loosening them.

"Funny how we meet up like this," Vinnie said. "What a pleasant surprise you've brought for me."

"No, no," Teresa said again, her voice frantic. "I just need you to let me go. That's all you have to do. You can do whatever you want with her. I thought you'd be happy about that. Aren't you happy about that?"

As she spoke, Molly watched in horror as the bigger man pulled the smaller woman across the room. Teresa struggled valiantly, but she didn't appear to want to lose her footing. The only option she had to prevent Vinnie from pulling her out of the room was to play dead.

Molly suspected even Teresa's full weight wouldn't be enough to keep him from carrying her out. He wasn't a weak-looking man.

"What are you doing?" she asked. Her body was re-energized by what was going on. She was able to pull up from her position. She found she could get all the way to a standing position, but it was hard to stand up when her feet were tied so close to each other. "Let her go!" she cried out, her heart slamming in fear. "You let her go! Let her go! You have me. You don't need her anymore! Just let her go!"

She tried to give Teresa a look of confidence and strength. If Vinnie saw no need to have her around and didn't trust her not to talk, didn't that mean he was going to take her out?

Molly shuddered and tried to move forward, but the momentum set off her balance and she felt herself tipping over.

To her utter astonishment, Vinnie's hands were catching her and pushing her back to her feet.

She dropped to her knees for more steadiness and ended up toppling over so she was sitting sideways.

Vinnie was staring at her closely. When he was apparently satisfied that she was unharmed, he continued to push Teresa out the door. It was soon closed behind them. Molly twisted her neck to see what was behind him. She spotted a hallway, a dark gray wall, the edge of what might have been a door or railing... that was it. The door was closed.

She looked around. There was a window, but a long stretch of cardboard had been pulled over it, blocking the view from it. Molly could probably pull the cardboard down, but she suspected they were not on the bottom floor. In fact, she imagined they were on one of the middle or top floors of that ratty hotel/apartment building she and Eddie had seen.

If that's where she was, Molly could be a bit hopeful. The only thing to do at that point was concentrate on loosening the bindings that kept her hands behind her back. Her feet were tied with crafting twine. She'd used that kind of twine in her crafts over the years. It was nearly impenetrable. Even sharp scissors had a hard time with that type of twine.

But there was something she knew about that particular twine. It worked better when it was twisted around and around itself. When tied, it tended to slip free. Even a double knot was unreliable.

She began to work her hands around, feeling the twine until she found the loops. She was gratified that whoever tied her up didn't know that.

As she worked the loops, imagining them in her mind so she could "see" what she was doing, she thought about the accomplice. Teresa seemed a viable option, but would she be creepy and clever enough to devise a kidnapping plan behind Vinnie's back?

Was this place hers or his? Was she behind it all, or was he? Was there yet another person in the mix? The one from the tires, keying, fire incidents?

She lifted her eyes and looked around her. The walls were also gray, like outside the room, but the color was lighter. There were no pictures on the walls at all. No furniture in the room. Paper blowing around that looked like receipts, old newspapers and magazine pages. There were a few dust tumbleweeds, loose cobwebs that fluttered every time someone opened or closed the door.

Molly wished Eddie was there to help her. She was glad he wasn't a prisoner with her.

Her only hope was if he remembered where the old apartment building they'd seen was located. If he remembered that, he would find her.

Chapter Thirty-Four

Eddie was more than a little surprised that he didn't see Molly when he went to work that morning. He'd started making it a point to be at work five minutes before normal so he could "walk past" her in the hallway as she went to work. Then they could walk the rest of the way together.

He wasn't immediately worried, but something was eating at him. If she was not the woman he thought she was, she might have skipped out in the middle of the night with those jewels Steven had given them. He was convinced she wasn't that kind of woman.

But did he really know her that well?

He didn't wait long. It was just a little after eight when he pressed the 'up' elevator button and waited patiently, his heart pounding for it to reach the ground level. He stepped on when the doors opened and tapped the '2' button a little harder than he intended.

He wasn't going to be angry. Not yet. He had to believe in her. Something else was wrong. Maybe she had a headache or was sick for some reason. Maybe she decided to sleep in because the treasure had been found and there was no need to worry anymore.

He got to her door and knocked three times. As soon as his hand hit the door and with each knock, it moved open a little more.

Eddie's heart nearly stopped. He pushed it open the rest of the way with his fingers and looked down the short, dark hallway that was open to the left, revealing the living room.

"Molly?" he called out. "Moll? Where are you? You decent? It's me, Eddie."

He expected her to call back to him. He wanted her to call back to him.

"Molly! Molly!"

With no return greeting, Eddie knew something was definitely wrong. He raced through the suite from room to room. Nothing was disturbed. There was no sign of a struggle. The window doors to the balcony were open and the curtains pulled aside.

Molly wasn't there.

Eddie ran back to the front door. Once there, he looked to his right, to a large wooden key with small hooks attached to it. Her car keys were hanging there. Eddie dropped his eyes to her purse, sitting on a small round white decorative table below the key.

"Oh, no..." he breathed. "No, no, no..."

The next moment, Eddie was racing down the hall to the elevator. In his mind, he went through the possible scenarios and who exactly he should contact at that moment. He decided to go to Steven first. Steven seemed to know people in the police. He could get someone on it quick.

But where would she have gone? She obviously didn't go on her own. She would have taken her personal items. At least her keys.

Maybe she got another threatening text! he thought frantically. He hadn't thought to look for her phone. If there was one thing he knew, it was that she would have her phone in her hand unless she was sleeping.

Eddie chided himself for being a terrible detective. He hadn't looked for the most important item someone might have—Molly's phone—and he hadn't looked at her bed to see if it had been slept in. He tried to recall in his mind, but he'd been so concentrated on the open double glass doors, he hadn't even looked at the bed. If drawers had been left open, he would have noticed, but he didn't recall that either.

He would never have his own tv detective show, that was a fact.

He fought against the urge to go back and do a more thorough search. Getting to Steven and getting the authorities on top of the case was the most important thing right then. They would be better at looking for clues, anyway.

He raised his eyebrows to the secretary, Candy, who nodded at him. That was usually her sign that Steven was free to have visitors. It was only eight-forty-five. Steven was probably just getting his brain together for the workday.

Eddie knew a lot of people like that. Personally, he had no problem with mornings.

"Steven?" he said the man's name as soon as he opened the door.

Steven looked up expectantly. "Yes?"

"Molly is gone."

Steven was on his feet in less than a second. "What?"

Eddie knew Steven had heard exactly what he said. Instead of repeating himself, he expanded.

"I just went to her room and looked for her, because there really isn't any reason for her not to be in her office. She's not there. Her purse and her keys are but she's not. I didn't look for a cell phone. I didn't see any signs that she was forcibly taken. She might have been knocked out."

Steven's face was a beacon of concern. "All right. Let me call John at the station. See what he can do to help us. Probably not much. No signs of a struggle. Just her purse and cell phone there won't make a difference."

"If they can't help us," Eddie asked, "why get them involved? Let's you and me go back and search her room. Look for what I've missed. See if her phone is there and if she got any new texts. Any notes that were left behind. Anything you can see that I didn't see."

Steven's hand was hovering over his cell phone, which was on his desktop. His eyes were on Eddie. He nodded and picked up his phone.

"You make a good point. You and me, let's go back and look through the room. I'm gonna call John anyway because the earliest we get them involved, the better. If they want to wait forty-eight hours, we want that time to start quick, right? She is a grown woman. They aren't going to treat it like a kidnapping without good cause."

Eddie left the room with him and the two men hurried down the hall. "Don't you think the text messages are enough to show there's good cause for searching for her? As a hostage? I mean, she got one that said you're next. That doesn't get much clearer, does it?"

Steven looked thoughtful. "You're right." The look in his eyes changed when someone answered the phone. Eddie only gave the conversation half his attention. He was worried about Molly. More than he'd ever worried about another human being in his life. He realized I that moment he would walk a hundred miles to get to her if he knew she was waiting for him. He knew what men were saying when they talked about a girl that "got them through the war" and other extremely hard times.

"Okay," Steven said, pulling the phone from his ear and pushing the red end button. "John said he's gonna send a couple of uniforms over to look through the apartment. A detective isn't available right now, but they'll send one when they get time. John's pretty influential down there. He's got pull. Someone will come to help find her."

They were at the elevator, and more anxious than before, Eddie tapped his fingers together in anticipation of it opening. When the doors opened, he hopped on like they were going to suddenly close if he didn't hurry. Steven was right behind him and it was Steven who punched the number two button.

Neither said anything until they were in the apartment.

"I just went through real quick," Eddie said, going straight for the bedroom.

Steven raised his eyebrows when both men reached the door at the same time.

"You've been in here before?" Steven asked.

"I have," Eddie replied in a casual tone, walking through and gazing at the bed first thing. It looked untouched. It had not been slept in. "She was scared one night by a light out there. That night that you were informed, remember?"

Steven snorted. "How could I forget?"

"I was in here that night. Stayed the night. On the couch." He gave Steven a direct look. "Look. The bed hasn't been slept in. There's her cell phone." He went to the bedside table and picked up the phone.

He pressed his finger on the button, and the screen lit up. He was pleasantly surprised to see it was the picture they had taken with their sacks of gems, a picture of them all, holding the sacks and gems up in the air, big smiles on all their faces.

"It's password protected," he said, disappointed but not surprised.

"Okay," Steven said. "Let's try to figure it out."

Chapter Thirty-Five

Molly didn't know how long she'd been in the room. Maybe a few hours? Had she fallen asleep?

Her hands and feet were asleep, she knew that. She hadn't changed her position much since Vinnie took Teresa out. She hadn't heard a sound from the other rooms since the two had left either. She could only assume they had left the apartment altogether.

If that's where she was.

Molly wished she had a telepathic mind. She would send Eddie messages to remind him of the apartment building where they had seen Vinnie. If only he would remember.

She had managed to get up on her knees and stretch her aching back a few times. The floorboards underneath her were hard. It reminded her of the times she'd gone camping and how uncomfortable it was to sleep on the ground.

She'd been working on the loops of the twine and it was almost loose enough for her to pull her hands out without ripping all the skin off. Just a few more manipulations of her hands.

Just as Molly had expected, she was about to get pull one hand out from the twine binding when she heard a noise outside the door. Her heart plummeted to her stomach when she saw the doorknob turning. She was still on her knees and didn't want to sit down again. Her behind was hurting and her lower back stabbed with pain.

The door flew open and Vinnie stepped in. She tried to see around him again, but saw nothing more than she had before.

She tried to add to what she could see and form some kind of picture in her mind, but it was impossible.

She didn't know what the inside of the apartments looked like in that building. She had no frame of reference other than her own suite at the Inn.

"What do you want?" she asked.

Vinnie came directly over and knelt in front of her. She was surprised to see a regretful look on his face. He didn't say anything at first, which made Molly more nervous than anything else. She just stared at him.

"You really don't know what's going on, do you?" she asked, her voice soft and quiet.

His eyes sharpened and the corners of his lips turned down. "I didn't know you would be here, no. I didn't bring you here, no. But I know what's going on. You have my treasure and I want it."

Molly's heart quaked in her chest. "How do you know we've got the treasure?" she asked.

His face changed again. "You know about it, then."

"Of course I know about it," Molly replied. "Your other hostage told me about it. She said you want it."

Vinnie threw back his head and laughed. The response was so unexpected, Molly was stabbed with a jolt of fear. He was crazy. There was little to nothing someone could really do to protect themselves against a lunatic. They proved to be unpredictable. Molly had seen enough true crimes shows to know that.

She had stopped messing with her twined arms but resumed as softly as possible, trying to get the final loop loosened.

"Steven is a very generous man," she said urgently. "He'd give you some of the gems. You wouldn't have to worry about a thing for the rest of your life."

Vinnie tilted his head to the side, his black eyes on hers. "You know who I am?"

Molly's heart raced, and her blood turned to ice. "Do you know who I am?" she asked. The next moment, she was silently chiding herself for provoking him.

"I know who you are," he snapped at her. "Do you know who I am?"

"I know who you are, yes," she repeated his words back to him. "You're Vinnie LaBrock. Eddie told us you'd been snooping around. We just don't know why."

"You do!" he yelled in her face, sweeping her with a wash of alcohol breath. "You know I want that treasure and all of it!"

Molly closed her eyes. "I know that. But why would you harass and threaten Teresa and then kidnap her and hold her hostage? She doesn't know anything about the treasure or where it was!"

"You have what's legally mine. My father discovered the treasure was there many, many years ago! He wrote a book about it."

Molly nodded. "Along with others. If he knew where it was, why didn't he go get it?"

"He tried," Vinnie replied, his face turning red. He was still uncomfortably close. Molly wondered why he didn't seem to mind being a foot and a half from her face. "He couldn't find it. And I didn't kidnap Teresa. She came here on her own. She got you and brought you here and made herself up to look like that. She's gonna blackmail me."

Molly took some comfort from his words. If Teresa had a chance to sue him, she must be alive. But on the other hand, if she really was the mastermind behind all this, why should Molly care what Vinnie did with her?

"So she's the one who was keying Steven's car and the fire in Paula's kitchen?"

Vinnie shook his head. "All her. I just wanted to dig up the treasure. That's all I've ever wanted."

"Then why aren't you letting me out of here?" Molly's hope for rescue might come sooner than she expected. She wiggled her hands, aware that she was almost free as it was.

Vinnie lowered his eyes and his head, shaking it. "I can't. She'll kill me if I do."

Molly frowned. "She's going to sue you *and* kill you? You really aren't in control here, are you?"

Vinnie looked around. "She invaded my home. This room was just a spare. No furniture, you see. I was going to use it for storage until I found my dad's treasure. I tried to put some time in between every time I came up to dig."

Molly was confused. She pulled her eyebrows together, watching the man as he pushed to his feet and went to the window. She was stunned to see him stand, facing it, as if he could see out. "She put this darn cardboard up, too. She don't care about what other people want. She just does whatever she wants."

Molly was stunned to realize Teresa really *was* the one behind all of it.

"Did she tell you about the treasure, or did you tell her?" Molly asked.

"I told her, of course. She didn't know about it until I told her. I was looking for it and she took over! She just came in and took over! I wish I'd never laid eyes on that girl! Look what trouble I'm in now!"

Molly almost felt sorry for Vinnie. All he'd needed to do was come up and talk to Steven about the treasure. He would have been included along with the rest of them. But now he was insistent that the treasure was all his, and he was a party to kidnapping.

He was indeed in a lot of trouble.

She felt sympathy for him.

"I'll tell Steven you had nothing to do with the kidnapping," she said, "but you've done a lot of trespassing and you've been caught on camera because we do have CCTV, you know."

He looked devastated. He leaned back against the wall, one hand pushed against her forehead.

"This isn't gonna be good," he said, shaking it, rubbing his skin with his fingers.

"No," she said softly. "It isn't."

Chapter Thirty-Six

"Vincent LaBrock," Steven said, staring down at his phone. "435 Morningside lane, Vinton, Va." He glanced over at Eddie. "Let's go check there. John isn't gonna be able to send anyone to his house. That's more of a detective thing to do than uniform."

Eddie shook his head. "Nah, I doubt that. They could send a uniform over to do a welfare check. They've done it for less reasons than this."

"They won't be able to look for her there, though. Don't they need a reason for that?"

"I don't know," Eddie replied honestly. He wished he did. He'd never entertained the idea of becoming a law officer even once in his life. He had no clue what the codes meant and didn't know procedures—proper or otherwise.

"Let's go anyway," Steven said. "I want to find her."

Eddie understood that. He nodded.

"Let's take my truck," Steven said. "It stands out and gets attention. That way we don't get in trouble for going over there."

"You don't want to go unnoticed? We could take my Toyota and get no attention at all."

It was then that Steven turned a grin to Eddie so he'd know the man had been trying to be funny.

"Yeah, that's better. If you don't mind the extra gas."

Eddie shrugged. "No, that's fine. I've got a nearly full tank."

An hour later, they were pulling up in front of 435 Morningside lane. It was a trailer. There were bottles and other debris scattered around the front lawn area, which was about ten feet of brown and green grass spots, with a narrow concrete sidewalk straight down the middle.

Eddie looked around him as he got out of the driver's seat. There were more trailers around them, in a long straight row on their right and a haphazard row on the left, as if the people on that side couldn't decide who had how much yard space in between. Some had awnings while others had full decks built on.

They weren't in the best of shape, but it looked like some of Vinnie's neighbors were at least trying.

"Not a bad place to live," he mumbled. "But not a good place, either."

Steven shook his head. "I don't have to be wealthy to say I don't want to live in a place like this."

Eddie grinned at his friend. "I guess it's a good thing you don't have to. You can stick with your television coming out of your walls."

Steven chuckled.

The two men walked around the outside of the trailer, making a circle around it. They were barely able to get around the back end of the trailer because of the overgrown brush in their way.

But they managed with only a few cuts to the face and arms.

"You wanna try to go in?" Eddie asked.

"Well, we aren't leaving without knocking on the door," Steven replied with a light chuckle.

They went up the steps to the door of the trailer and knocked on it.

Silence.

Steven looked at Eddie as he knocked a second time. "Is it against the law to go in a house if the door is unlocked?" he asked.

Eddie blinked at him. "I don't know. I don't think so," he said, "but don't quote me on that."

"You're gonna get in as much trouble as me if you come in." Steven had to laugh.

"Yeah, yeah. Give it a try already."

Steven turned the knob without hesitation and pushed the door open. He cocked his head to the side, hesitated and then called out, "That you, Vinnie? It's Steven Smith from the Oceanside Inn!"

He looked back at Eddie. "You hear that?"

Before Eddie could deny hearing whatever sound it was Steven claimed to hear, he was in the trailer, looking around, picking up newspapers and then dropping them with a look of revulsion on his face.

"I don't think there's anyone here," he said, glancing around at the empty silence.

"Yeah, I think you're right about that."

"What do you want to do? Go to the police?"

Steven stood for a moment, looking around.

Eddie was devastated that they hadn't found Molly in the trailer. He distracted himself by talking to Steven. "Did Molly get a chance to tell you what she discovered about that address that was texting her?"

Steven gave him a confused look. "What do you mean?" he asked.

"I'm talking about that last message she got. She looked at it closely and said that it was sent from an email address. She didn't tell you that?"

Steven shook his head. "No. What's the difference? What's so special about that?"

"Well, she said the others all came from a text number, probably a burner phone, maybe even a new one each time. But that last one came from an email. And it seemed to have a lot to do with Sabatino LaBrock."

"That's pretty interesting," Steven admitted, nodding, standing near the door, probably so the smell of dust and dirt wasn't right in his face. "But can we leave now? There's nothing here for us to see. The ladies aren't here. There's no attic, and we'd hear and see them if they were in the crawlspace under the trailer."

"True." Eddie walked toward the door. His fourth step, his shoe jammed into a board that was sticking up a little from the floor. He looked down at it and noticed it looked warped. He narrowed his eyes and leaned down, putting two fingers underneath the warped board and prying it out easily.

In the hole underneath, he saw a small book neatly placed between the floorboards.

"Well, well, well," he said. "What do you know?"

He leaned down and picked it up.

"Don't you go and tell me Vinnie's the kind of guy who keeps a journal of all his misdoings."

"You never know. He could be like Grue from Despicable Me. You know, soft and lovable on the inside but tough and mean on the outside."

Steven laughed, the worry in his voice still there. "I think you and Molly should get along just fine if you're talking about Despicable Me. She loves that movie and the ones after it, too."

Eddie had to chuckle. It was nice to know that little tidbit of information about Molly. He would place it in his memory, never to let it go.

"When we find her, I'll be sure to take her out for nachos and Despicable Me if it comes back in the theaters."

"Wait long enough and there might be another one to see," Steven mumbled, his eyes dropping to the book. "So what it is? What's in it?"

Eddie had been talking, distracted, so when he glanced down at the book he was flipping through, he noticed it was filled with numbers. Different sequences of numbers. Strange words written in margins and in places around the notebook. Words that didn't seem to fit together until he realized what it might have been.

"I think this is a journal of where Vinnie has looked for the treasure," he remarked, tossing the little book to Steven, who snatched it neatly from the air.

He opened it to a middle page and scanned the numbers and words in his mind. "I don't know what the words mean, but the numbers could easily be longitude and latitude. They do look like directing numbers, though. Like a map written in words and numbers instead of visual pictures."

"Exactly!" Eddie stated firmly. "I don't know why anyone would just not use GPS when they are looking for anything anymore."

"I'm sure that's because these kinds of things aren't on GPS. And when would his pop or his grandfather or any of those relatives wrote the directions to the treasure? They didn't have GPS, did they?"

"Once again, you're right," Eddie said. He looked around for the last time and shook his head. "Let's get out of here. No need to even be in here. What are we gonna do now?"

Steven continued looking through the book as they walked down to the car. He slid into the passenger seat and looked over at Eddie as he put on his seat belt.

"I think the next place we should go is Teresa Knox's apartment. You haven't been there, but I have. I want to look around in there." Steven settled in, turning the book in his direction, his thumb holding it open to a certain spot. "Look there." He pointed at a row of numbers on one page. It was toward the end of the book, one of the last entries. There were four or five numbers with the letters TK running down the side.

Eddie started the car, glancing at the letters and then Steven himself. "Teresa Knox," he said.

"Exactly," Steven responded with a nod.

Chapter Thirty-Seven

After Vinnie left, Molly continued to untie herself. She pulled the last loop free and felt the rope slide from her wrists. Immediately untying her ankles, she got to her feet and stretched high up in the air, lifting up on her tiptoes. She felt her aching bones pull and her muscles stretch.

With a great sigh, Molly went to the window with the cardboard and pulled it down, pushing her fingers in between the board and the window frame.

She pulled on it until it separated and she could see behind it. Unfortunately, she only saw pitch darkness, which told her either the window had been boarded up or removed completely, leaving only the frame there.

She tugged harder on the cardboard until it came off completely, hanging by just one corner. She yanked on it hard until it came off and floated to the ground nearby. She stared at the windowsill, which was absolutely huge. She hadn't seen any windows of this size or shape in the apartment building where they'd followed Vinnie.

With a panicked jolt, Molly realized she couldn't be in that apartment building. There were other people living there, even if it was in bad shape. She hadn't heard anyone above her walking around. In fact, Molly hadn't heard anyone in what she suspected had been at least twelve hours or so.

Vinnie was the only one she saw or heard since Teresa had left. The gray room beyond the door looked like nothing more than another room to her. A railing. A wall. No pictures. No decorations. Nothing that could stand out.

She had no idea where she was.

That thought made her stomach turn. How was she going to get out of here?

She crossed to the door and was astonished that it wasn't locked. She almost hesitated to open it, afraid that Vinnie and Teresa would be standing on the other side, ready to shoot her down for trying to escape.

She pulled in a deep breath and tried to put her fears aside. She closed her eyes for a moment and yanked the door open.

The room on the other side was barren. An old, dusty, round rug was in the middle of the floor. There were various furnishings—all covered in dust—placed around the room.

It was also empty of people. Molly's stomach growled loudly, and she instinctively looked for a kitchen. She saw it, but it was obvious there was nothing along the lines of food in that place. The other windows in the house had been boarded up, but there was one to the right of the front door that had some small spaces in between the crossed boards, revealing the outside of the house she was in.

She crossed to it quickly and put her fingers up on the board, squinting through the diamond shaped opening.

Her eyebrows pulled together in confusion. All she saw was trees. Nothing but trees. Was she back at the lake? Were these trees around the Inn?

Her chest squeezed with anxiety. What would she be doing back there? Why would Teresa bring her back to the Inn?

"No," she said aloud, shaking her head. "I can't be back at the Inn. Vinnie said he owned the place and that he had an extra room. If I'm at the lake, that's one thing. But Vinnie doesn't own any part of the Inn."

Molly was aware she was practically trying to convince herself. She wondered silently if talking aloud to oneself was a sign of insanity. That's what she'd heard, she was sure.

She went to the front door and examined it. There was no way it was just going to open to her like the room she'd come from. She put her hand on the knob and turned it. It turned freely, but the door didn't budge. Her eyes flipped up to the deadlock above the knob. She touched it, tracing the lock with one finger.

It needed a key. From the inside and the outside. And it was locked tight. If she escaped, it wouldn't be through that door.

She thought for a moment and then moved back to the window with the crossed boards in front of it. She put her hands up where she could on the board in front of the other one. She yanked, jerked, pulled, but the board wouldn't budge. It couldn't have been that she was just too weak. It seemed like there had to be some other reason.

She examined the boards more closely and saw what looked like glue residue on the edges of the board closest to the wall. They were secure and in place. She wasn't getting out of there of her own volition. She would have to wait for someone to come back and open the door.

Molly turned in a slow circle, looking at the drab, dusty house. No one had lived there for many years. She couldn't imagine it being occupied at all, but if it was standing, she was sure it was at one point.

She imagined the key sliding in the lock. Where would she go? Should she hide and jump out at whoever came through the door? Should she search for a cell phone or a regular land line? Sweeping her eyes around the room, she could tell the last time this place was lived in, it probably did have land lines. Computers were probably still huge boxes that took up an entire office space.

The house was so still. The air was stale. Fresh air had only been allowed recently, most likely, with Teresa suddenly putting the shack to good use. That's what Molly called the place in her mind. It couldn't be more than a shack, with one bedroom, a small bathroom with a narrow yellow bathtub, a one row of cabinets and counters, kitchen and a living room.

What was it, six-hundred square feet?

"Probably go for a thousand a month in New York," she murmured.

If she waited long enough, either Vinnie or Teresa would be showing their faces. What would she do? Should she pounce or hide? Maybe she could throw water in their faces? Maybe salt or flour or something. Distract them and run out and jump in their car and drive away...

She could picture it. But a quick turn of the faucet proved there was no running water—which she didn't really expect anyway—and the cupboards were bare. There was no flour or salt to blind her captors, so she could escape.

So what could she do? Was there anything at all in the house that could be used as a defensive weapon?

She swept her eyes from one side of the living room to the other. Her stomach was beginning to ache. She put one hand over it, moaning.

"Stop it, Molly," she mumbled. "Food will be on the way. Just shut up."

She pulled in a deep breath. She hoped food would be on the way.

It was hard to wrap her brain around the fact that Teresa was the one behind it all. And if that was true, and this house was Vinnie's, there would be no tie to her if she was found where she was.

Desperate for a way out of the house, Molly began closely examining each window, even the small one in the kitchen she likely wouldn't fit through. It was above the sink, so it would be quite an ordeal to go through it if she had to.

She prayed as hard as she could—for strength and guidance and a way out.

Chapter Thirty-Eight

The first thing Eddie noticed when he and Steven got to Teresa's apartment was that it had been cleaned up. Steven mentioned it as soon as they stepped out of the Toyota.

"Look at that," he said, gesturing to the clear front stoop. Eddie remembered him mentioning the mail was piling up. "I guess she came back. Wonder where she's been?"

Eddie could hear the suspicion and doubt in Steven's voice. He looked at the man as they walked up the sidewalk to the front stoop.

"You ever notice anything off about the woman before all this? What did you do when she reported the harassing texts?"

Eddie was surprised to see Steven's face flush bright red.

"I don't think we did enough to address the issue, I can tell you that," he said stiffly. He stopped halfway up the sidewalk, his eyes on the front door of the apartment. "She was a nice lady. Capable and competent at her job. But when the texts started..." He shook his head. "There was something about them that made me feel like she was getting them from an ex-boyfriend who just wanted to mess with her. They were like... like that movie where the kids kept finding notes all over, threatening them. I didn't feel like it was my responsibility to do anything about it. Not to an excess anyway. It was her business. Had nothing to do with the Inn."

"But that changed when she left and Molly started getting the texts?"

"Yes," he replied, nodding. "Molly has nothing in her life or her past that would subject her to something like that. And telling her to leave the Inn?" He shook his head. "None of it made sense."

They started walking again, but remained slow. "So are you saying that when you got your tires slashed and your car keyed and Paula's kitchen was caught on fire, you didn't associate those things with the texts Teresa was getting?"

Steven nodded. Eddie could see he'd impressed Steven with his insight. He looked like he regretted it at the same time.

"And suddenly you and Paula and Jack were safe from sabotage?"

"Yes. That's the way it seemed. Suddenly the focus seemed to be on Molly."

Eddie thought about it for a moment.

"And Molly was the only person in your gang who didn't have something happen to her. Except Andy, but he's not here anymore, anyway."

Steven nodded again. They had reached the front door of Teresa's apartment and he reached out to knock. "It's almost like Teresa told the person who was texting her that she'd left and that he should bother Molly instead," he said.

Eddie had a different view in mind. He waited with an anxious heart to see if Teresa would come to the door, but he heard nothing on the other side. "It sounds more to me like Teresa wasn't important enough to get the texts. Why would she be getting them in the first place? She's not a member of your group, is she?"

Steven shook his head. "No. Never has been."

"Then why did she get them in the first place? What did they say? Did they tell her to leave or relinquish some kind of ownership in the Inn?"

"I don't remember what her texts said," Steven admitted. "Like I said, she wasn't important like that to me. She was important..." He was quick to follow up his initial statement, "just not important in that way."

"I understand what you mean. She should have had friends and family supporting and helping her, whereas you were her boss. Had you even met her?"

"Not other than the interview to be hired."

Eddie nodded. He looked back and forth at the windows on either side of the door. "She might have been here and cleaned up and all that, but she's definitely not here right now."

"I really want to get in there," Steven murmured under his breath.

"I know the feeling," Eddie said. "But what can we do? We'll be breaking the law if we go in there."

Steven pulled his eyebrows together and cocked his head. He rolled his eyes up to the sky.

"What's that?" he asked sharply.

Eddie raised his eyebrows. "What?" he asked.

"You don't hear that? It sounds like a woman in pain. We should get in there and make sure everyone is okay!"

To Eddie's utter astonishment, Steven moved down the porch to the window to the right of the door. It was cracked open slightly. Steven slipped his hand in where it was open and deftly spun the knob until the window was all the way open.

"You aren't getting through that window, Steven," he pointed out. Steven was much too big.

His boss turned and gave him a look. "If we don't find Molly, this Vinnie character might kill her, Eddie. He might have already killed Teresa. Just because we have suspicions about her doesn't mean she isn't an innocent victim. Vinnie's or not. We have to get in. We have to make sure she's okay. If we can save those women, we'll be forgiven for breaking into her house to find clues."

Eddie hated that Steven's reasoning was sound. He hated to even think about breaking the law, much less going into someone's house illegally. But what else could he do?

Steven was right. And by the way he was looking at Eddie, it was obvious Eddie was the one who could fit through the window. Steven was just waiting for him to do it.

"Ugh," he groaned, walking slowly toward the window. "You know what they say about the best intentions, right?"

Steven nodded. "I'm worried about both women, Eddie. Please do this. I'll take all the blame. We aren't in there to steal anything. We're just worried about Molly... and Teresa."

Eddie sucked in a deep breath. He stepped up to the small window and put his hand on opposite sides. It was easier than he'd thought it would be to hoist himself up and over the windowsill. Once he was in the apartment, he landed on a couch and bounced off to the floor. He went to the door and unlocked it from the inside, sliding the handle lock to the side-side position.

Steven came in and both men began looking around in silence.

Eddie noticed how quiet the house was—how still the air was. It took a moment before he realized why it felt that way. It didn't appear there was any electricity on in the apartment. The telltale buzz and hum of electronic appliances in the kitchen and central air units was missing.

It was as quiet as a tomb.

"I'm going to look in her room," Steven said. "Why don't you come with me so that if this plan goes awry, like if a neighbor saw us come in that way, we won't be accused of stealing anything later?"

Eddie frowned. "I don't like the sound of that. We could be in a lot of trouble if someone saw us."

"Relax," Steven replied. "I looked around and I don't think anyone was watching. I can't be a hundred percent sure, but I don't think anyone can. And if the cops get called, remember, they know me. I will tell them the situation and they will understand. Probably tell me to stop trying to investigate things on my own. They've tried to tie my hands before, but I always come out on top because I'm doing the right thing. I'm on the right side of the law. And I have God directing my steps. At least I hope that's what I'm doing. Trying not to make any decisions in my life without consulting Him first, you know?"

Eddie didn't really know. He was a follower of Jesus and believed wholeheartedly that God was alive and working on behalf of all His children, but it wasn't something that occupied his mind very often. He certainly didn't have the ability or knowledge to "consult Him" first. Maybe if he spent enough time around Steven, he would learn to do that.

He followed his boss into the bedroom, stopping at the doorway. It was a mess. Clothes strewn everywhere, drawers sitting open, magazines, mail and other papers spread all over the floor.

"Wonder what happened here," Steven said, bending at the knees and picking through some of the clothes. "These all look like things a woman would wear. I mean, why would she leave these behind? Maybe Vinnie was looking for something. A treasure map or something. She definitely didn't go digging around the boatyard. She's never been anywhere near where we found the treasure, as far as I know."

"Here we go," Eddie said, his eyes falling on a book sticking out from under several others. It looked similar to the one he'd found in the trailer belonging to Vinnie. "What's this?"

He bent and plucked it from under the other books. "Looks like another ledger. A treasure hunting ledger."

He opened the book and scanned the front page. A chill ran up his spine when he spotted something completely unexpected on the inside of the front cover. He turned the book around and showed Steven.

It was a small simple map with several street names and a literal X marking the spot.

Above it was an address.

Chapter Thirty-Nine

Molly had grown bored quickly. She could only nap so much. So when the light outside started to go dim, and she was wide awake in a huge empty house, growing hungrier and thirstier by the minute, she began to think about her options. How long could she survive without food or water? It was water that concerned her the most. She hadn't gotten to the point where she would drink the water from the toilet yet. The house being abandoned so long ago made Molly think that water might not be "good" anymore. Sure, it would taste horrible, but she could only imagine the kind of bacteria that was likely growing in it.

She hadn't even looked at it yet. In her stressed state, she had yet to feel the need to use the bathroom. Plus, she had no food or liquid in her stomach to dispel.

Molly's thoughts began to wander. She prayed for a few minutes and then would be distracted by wayward thoughts, some panicked, some not. She ended up sitting on the floor in the very middle of the round rug, looking at the front door, waiting for someone to come through.

"Someone will come eventually," she whispered to herself.

But what if no one did? Teresa didn't need to come back. What did Molly have that she wanted? Nothing. What did Molly have that Vinnie wanted? Nothing. It was simply an extra room in a house owned by Vinnie that could very well have been in Canada for all she knew. Molly had no idea how long she'd been unconscious. She didn't know what day it was.

She knew she was starving and thirsty.

The quiet of the house made every sound amplified in Molly's ears. So when she heard a rustling sound coming from outside, she knew it was likely a person. She knew from having grown up hunting with her brothers and father in the woods of Virginia the sound of a deer or other four-legged animal when walking through the woods. It was very much different from a human.

The rustling sound continued, and she heard voices. She struggled to hear a female voice and was up on her feet, approaching the door a second later. She pressed her ear up to the boards crossing over the window and peered through the diamond shaped opening. She didn't see anyone, but that wouldn't stop her from trying to look.

Her heart nearly stopped when she heard someone call out, "Steven! Over here!"

It was Eddie's voice. The men sounded like they were in front of the house.

In one frantic motion, Molly flew to the front door of the house and began beating on it with her fists, screaming for Eddie and Steven to help get her out.

She kept up the noise for about a minute before stopping so she could hear what their reaction was or if they'd even heard her. If only the holes in the boards over the windows were big enough for her hand. She would put it through the glass if she thought it would help her be rescued.

"Molly?" She heard both men call out her name at the same time.

A fist beat on the other side of the door.

"Molly! Are you in there? Let us in! Are you there?"

Molly turned in a circle, searching the room with panicked eyes. She had to let them know it was her, and she needed their help. The door was thick. She couldn't tell whether Eddie was just knocking because that's the way to get a door to open or if he'd heard her calling out and banging.

She beat on the door again, yelling, "Can you hear me? Can you hear me?"

She heard nothing for a moment and then murmured voices.

Molly had to assume they couldn't hear her. She turned around again and headed for the kitchen. There had to be something she could use in there. Something... anything...

She yanked open the drawers that were slid shut. They were all empty except the third one and the only thing in the drawer was an old metal butter knife that had rusted on one side.

Molly chewed on her bottom lip, running her finger along the dull edge of the knife. Her eyes moved around the room. In a last ditch effort to get the men to hear her, she would have to break the glass in the only part of the window she could.

It wasn't a big area, but she didn't need a large hole to put her voice through it. The window she wanted to use was at the front of the house beside the door. It was the best place to do it, in her opinion.

She returned to the window with the crossed boards. Without a moment's hesitation, she tapped the glass in the diamond-shaped holes and smashed out all the glass. Knowing that alone was enough to get the attention of the men, she went ahead and yelled through the hole she'd made. "I'm here! Come in and get me!"

At first she was certain what she "heard" was stunned silence.

A second later, Eddie's face appeared on the other side of the window. All she could see were his eyes and then an eye and a nose and then a nose and mouth.

"Eddie!" she yelled. "Oh, Eddie, you've got to get me out of here."

"I'll get you out!" he called back, astonishment in his voice. "I can't believe you... you're right here! I can't believe it! Steven! We gotta get her out of there."

"We're coming for you, Moll!" Steven yelled out. "We're coming for you! Just hang tight. Are you hurt? Did they hurt you?"

"No, they didn't hurt me!" Molly was stunned just a moment later to realize the men had used the word "we." "Wait, you know about Teresa?"

"You know about her?" Steven asked as Eddie disappeared from her line of vision. "Is she a part of this? Good guy or bad guy?"

"She's the one who brought me here. I don't think she expected Vinnie to come here, though. He looked surprised when he was here. How did you find me?"

"Girl put the address in a book we found in her apartment."

Molly frowned. That seemed a little too dumb for someone as smart as Teresa.

"You see anything about a bomb in that book?" she asked.

"What are you talking about?" Steven asked in an edgy voice.

"I'm just thinking Teresa's been trying to take out our group and the two of us going at once would be a bonus for her, don't you think?"

Steven snorted. "I *think* we need to trust God will get us out of this. She might be clever. But she's not *that* clever. She has no way of knowing we found that book with pretty singular directions here. She'd have to be following us and setting clues ahead of us somehow. Doubt she's a time-shifter."

Molly chuckled.

At that moment, Eddie reappeared, pushing Steven out of the way. Their boss pretended to be stumbling, but when he righted himself, it was obvious he had never lost control.

"You stand back, Molly!" he called out.

Molly ducked and hurried away from the window, unsure of what Eddie had found that would go through the door with such violence he wanted her to stand back.

A moment later, she found out.

Chapter Forty

Eddie had taken notice of the storage shed as soon as they stepped onto the property. When he got over his astonishment that Molly was trapped inside the house, he had to run back to it and look for a tool to get inside.

The shed was mostly empty and the tools that were left behind looked so old, Eddie suspected they would turn to dust if he tried to remove them from where they were hanging on a wide pegboard.

He had turned in a half circle and spotted the sledgehammer propped up against the wall in the corner.

Now he stood in front of a glass window boarded up on the other side, prepared to smash his way through.

He pulled the hammer back as far as he could, rocking his body to brace himself for the impact he would feel from the sledgehammer meeting the solid wood. This was wood and glass, though. A sledgehammer could go through a wall, through concrete, if need be.

He was about to swing the hammer when he heard, "Wait!"

He almost fell over backwards. He turned in amazement and saw Vinnie running toward him. The man's long coat was flapping around his legs. He had one arm up in the air. His eyes were wide and wild and his hair flopped all over his head.

"What are you doing?" he yelled, more upset than angry. "You can't do that to my window! Have you lost your mind?"

Eddie dropped the sledgehammer, stunned to see Vinnie running up to them like he didn't know he had a hostage inside his house. Surely he knew Molly was there. They already knew he was tied to Teresa and the crimes being committed at the Inn. Why now was he acting innocent and clueless?

"We might be wondering the same thing about you," Steven said, stepping out from the side of the house where he'd been hiding so the glass wouldn't cut him up if it came back out through the hole Eddie was about to make. Eddie could tell he was using his long legs to get in between Eddie and Vinnie as the other man got closer.

"You can't do that," Vinnie said frantically. "This is my house. You can't bust into it like that."

"You're holding a hostage in there!" Eddie growled. "A woman I care about! You kidnapped her and brought her here and she doesn't even have anything you want!"

He swiftly moved around Steven and pushed his chest into Vinnie so the thin man had to back up a little to get away from him. Vinnie looked surprised, which did more to calm Eddie down than anything else.

"Why are you surprised?" he asked vehemently. "You have to know she's in there."

"I know, I know," Vinnie replied, his voice weak and mouse like. He had reached into the pocket of his coat and pulled out a set of keys. He was going through them, giving Eddie a look like he was distracting Vinnie from finding the right key.

Vinnie stepped up onto the porch right in front of the door, and flanked by Steven and Eddie, pushed the key into the lock with shaking hands.

Eddie couldn't believe he was listening to Vinnie mumbling under his breath, "Gonna just bust right into my house, right through the window! Destruction! Not even his property!"

As soon as the lock was turned, Eddie twisted the doorknob and shoved the door open.

He pushed Vinnie out of the way as the man protested. All he wanted to do was get in to where Molly was.

She looked delighted, throwing her arms up in the air. She didn't look much worse for wear and he was a little shy to be seeing her in her silk pajamas.

"He took you last night from your bed?" Eddie asked, enveloping her in his arms, plunging his face into her dark hair. "I can't believe that. I can't believe it."

"No, it wasn't Vinnie," Molly said. He pulled away from her, examining her face. He cupped her cheeks in his hands. She had her eyes behind him and he twisted his neck to see Steven was holding Vinnie like a big cop might hold a pickpocket by the arm. Steven looked surprised and loosened his grip on the man, eventually letting go. "It was Teresa. Teresa Knox. She's the one behind all this stuff that's been happening. She took me from my room last night, Eddie, but not while I was sleeping. And yeah, it's a good thing I wasn't sleeping without clothes on."

"What an awful thought," Eddie replied with a nod. He was still holding her close. He wanted to kiss her. He didn't know if he could resist doing just that for much longer. She had filled up his heart to the very brim. He wanted to give her everything she could ever want.

His feelings overwhelmed him, and he had to hug her tight again.

"I'm so glad you're all right."

Now Molly hugged him back. She had been waiting to make sure no one hurt Vinnie before she could explain. She hadn't really explained much, not to Eddie's satisfaction, anyway. But he had a feeling that was coming.

"We really need to get you out of here," Steven said, lifting one hand to wave them over. "It's not clean in here. You need to get dressed. Let's get you back home."

Molly and Eddie moved to go past him and out the front door. Vinnie acted like he was going out the door first, but Steven grabbed him by the shoulder so he couldn't go out.

"You're not going anywhere without us," Steven said. "I want to hear what you have to say for yourself. You aren't completely innocent in this, you know."

Eddie stopped and watched the men. If Steven needed his help, he wanted to be ready to give it.

Vinnie looked like a beaten dog being threatened with a new roll of newspaper.

"I didn't want this to happen... none of this!" he exclaimed. "It's all that girl's fault. She took over!"

Molly lifted her head when he said that, looking at Eddie. "That's what he told me, too. And just like that. I really think Teresa might have forced Vinnie to get involved. I never knew she was a control freak, but I think she is. Criminal mastermind? Maybe not. But I bet she's a real control freak and likes pushing everyone around."

"She can do that behind bars just fine," Steven had the answer for that.

"Truer words were never spoken," Eddie said, nodding. He moved his eyes to Vinnie. "So you can either be dropped off at the police station for aiding and abetting and keeping the location of a kidnapped person hidden from authorities."

"I was bringing her food," Vinnie said in a small voice, holding his duffle bag out for them to see.

Eddie dropped his eyes to the bag for only a moment before looking back up at the dark-eyed man. "Well, good for you. I'm glad. But you've still done some pretty... nefarious things around here."

"I haven't!" Vinnie cried out. Eddie noted the hurt tone in his voice. "I just wanted my treasure. My father found it and I want it. I want it all."

"You aren't gonna get any of it," Steven growled, grabbing Vinnie by the back of his collar and shoving him toward the open doorway, "if you don't help us figure out how to track down and turn Teresa over to the authorities. You must know where she is."

Vinnie didn't say anything. Eddie, who was outside the little house, standing with Molly, turned his head to look at the man.

"You know where she is, don't you?"

Vinnie shook his head, keeping his head down. "I don't know where she is," he said.

"Then we'll take you to the police and you can explain how you aren't a part of this woman being held hostage inside *your house*."

Vinnie looked terrified, sliding his eyes to each of them before muttering, "Oh, all right. I know where she is. But she's gonna be mad at me for telling and you're gonna have to protect me. That woman is vicious."

Chapter Forty-One

Molly stepped out of the shower and wrapped herself in a towel. The bathrooms at the Inn were better than any she'd ever experienced, with a round, flat showerhead that dropped down like rain.

She was glad to be clean, but the honeybun and coffee she'd had didn't put a dent in her hunger.

She was hoping Eddie would take her out for a special dinner. Steak and potatoes. Nachos for appetizer. Maybe some fried pickles...

She sighed, thinking about all the food she wanted to consume, knowing she wouldn't be able to eat that much. It was a funny thought, and she left the bedroom a few minutes later, fully dressed and laughing at herself.

Eddie was in the living room of her suite. He was staring down at his phone, which he was holding in both hands with his thumbs poised up in the air above it so he could type at a moment's notice.

"Whatcha doing?" she asked, dropping down next to him on the couch and leaning over like a prying girlfriend.

He chuckled, backing away from her slightly but not turning the phone away so she couldn't see it. He was talking to Steven, who was currently in the process of leaving a message.

"Talking to the boss," he replied, moving back toward her when she wrapped her arms around his and hugged it to her chest.

"Well, tell him I said hi. But I need to get something good to eat and I'm not ready to make it myself. Let's go out."

"You're hungry now and you want to go and wait for someone in a restaurant to make you a good meal? How about I just make you one right here?"

"I don't have any meat thawed," Molly answered him, using a playful voice, "and I want to go out. That's why I put on my going out outfit. Do you like it?"

She hopped to her feet, feeling young again, twirling around for him to see her whole outfit, which was a basic baby blue dress that brought out her figure and the natural tan of her skin. She fluttered her eyelashes and giggled.

"You look beautiful, Molly. As usual. Don't know why you'd want to be with someone that looks like this." He stood up and ran his eyes down his body. Molly did the same thing, thinking his casual shirt and blazer with a pair of dark blue jeans looked fashionable on him.

"I like the way you look," she said. "I think you're very attractive. And if you put yourself down, you're essentially just insulting my taste and then we'll have to have our first argument."

Eddie's grin burst across his face. Molly couldn't help thinking he looked a ton cuter with that smile than without it. One side of his lips tended to lift higher than the other, creating a dimple in that cheek that made Molly want to cover him with kisses.

"Okay, well, I don't want to argue, but if that's what we argue about, I'll take it. May it never be anything more than that."

"It is kind of a petty thing to argue about. Anyway, please, can we get going? I'm so hungry!"

"Okay, okay!" Eddie laughed, hopping to his feet. "I heard ya. Never let it be said that I kept a woman from a meal she desperately wanted. And deserved, too."

As they went out the door, Molly glanced back at him. "Did the cops ever catch up with Teresa?" She'd been wondering about that through her entire shower. Since Eddie had been talking to Steven, she thought he was likely to know the ex-employee's fate. She would never rid her mind of the picture of misery Teresa made when Molly had thought she was a fellow prisoner.

"I think they have her in custody now," he said. "Steven didn't say, but he alluded to the fact that she'd been arrested."

Molly wondered why Steven didn't just come out and say it. If she'd been caught, surely he'd want them to know it. He hadn't warned them either, which made Molly even more confused. If Teresa was still out on her own, she might come and get Molly. Wouldn't she?

Molly pushed down a jolt of fear. She was with Eddie. They were going to be in a public place where Teresa wouldn't want to be. It wasn't like she was a sniper in the Army. She was a greedy, manipulative liar, but that was it. She had a criminal mind and used it to try to steal money from other people.

It was pathetic, Molly thought. No person should be foolish enough to use their high intelligence to commit crime instead of building up and prospering, creating businesses, and inventing things to make life easier. There was no doubt that Teresa was a highly intelligent person.

So why had she turned to the wrong side of the law?

"You will tell me if there is an update, won't you?" she asked, fishing in her purse for her key so she could lock the door behind her.

"You know I will, babe."

As they walked toward the elevator, Molly thought how amazing it felt to hear him call her "babe." He let the word roll right off his tongue. Such a smooth man—a charmer. She thought back to when she'd first met him. She'd been attracted to him right away, but he'd seemed so much shier then. He appeared to be more like a man who would rather stay in the shadows.

Now, as they walked through the foyer and the concourse of the main area in the Inn, he had his head held high. One hand was behind the small of her back, not really touching her but brushing lightly along her shirt when she moved. He didn't seem shy or insecure to Molly at all.

She had to feel a bit of pride about that. She knew that being with him made him feel that way. It was an amazing thing to know that someone else was proud just to be seen with her. She'd never felt anything like that before. It made her understand why so many people could be attention seekers.

"It was good to know that Vinnie didn't get in too much trouble," Molly said. "I'm not surprised Teresa got him wrapped up in her scheme. She's such an evil little manipulator, isn't she? And Vinnie's like this big teenager with no clue what's going on from one minute to the next."

Eddie grunted. Molly wondered why he made the sound until he spoke. "I liked him," he said bluntly. "I always hoped he wasn't involved in... well, the illegal stuff anyway. Obviously, him digging on Steven's property wasn't exactly a good thing.

But he didn't kidnap you. He didn't set fire to Paula's kitchen or key Steven's car."

"I'm glad I went back over that footage and realized that," Molly admitted. "I was ready to convict him myself, I'll tell you that."

Eddie nodded, casting her an affectionate glance. "I know you were. You really didn't like him from the moment you saw him on that screen, did you? You were convinced he was the one doing all that stuff."

Molly shrugged and gave him a nod. "I know now it wasn't him sending the texts. That's why I was so upset and scared. It was the texts that were freaking me out and when I saw him on the property, being all sketchy and everything, I just knew it was him. I was sure it was him sending them. And they scared me so much."

He wrapped an arm around her shoulders and gave her a kiss on the forehead.

"I'm going to give you the best dinner you've ever had in your life," Eddie said. "I'm gonna break the bank on the best and biggest steak there is and then we're gonna paint the town red."

"Red isn't my color, really," Molly joked as she slid into the passenger side of his Toyota. "Let's paint the town royal blue."

Eddie laughed as he got into the driver's seat. "You got it, honey. We'll paint the town blue."

Chapter Forty-Two

The restaurant was crowded. Molly knew something was up the moment she entered. There were too many people looking at her and smiling. Even members of the staff were watching her pass, whispering behind their hands.

Molly had never been terribly insecure. Shy was one thing but insecure she was not. When she saw them whispering that way, she studied the way they were standing and the looks in their eyes. They weren't trash-talking. They were excited about something.

Molly's stomach was turning over and over. As empty as it was, the motion wasn't good for her steadiness on her feet. She was glad to get to the special room Eddie had obviously paid for.

She entered the room and stopped almost immediately, causing Eddie to quickly side-step to keep from running her down. All her friends were sitting at the long table set up in the middle of the room. When she came in, they all raised their glasses at the same time. Eddie was given two, and he handed one to Molly. She looked at the clear bubbling liquid in the flute shaped glass.

"Champagne?" she asked in a lilted voice. She had champagne once before. It wasn't her favorite drink.

There was no way Eddie could know that. And she wasn't about to put a damper on his festivities. He had something planned, and she would make sure it worked out for him.

"Champagne," Eddie answered, nodding. "I hope you like it. I asked everyone to be here and the food, as you see, is already here. It just came, actually. I know what you like, so I got you your favorites."

Molly grinned. "Just what you promised?" She pretended to be very questioning of him. He grinned.

"Just what I promised."

He held out his hand to the place where she would sit. At her place sat a very large steak, steak cut fries, broccoli, a salad and... much to her amusement... a plate of nachos on the side.

"I think I've just gone to Heaven," she said, her mouth watering. "Either that or I'm about to be executed."

Eddie laughed. "Good Lord, can we not talk to the extremes here? I want to raise a toast to my lovely lady, Molly. Molly, since I met you, my life has changed a hundred and eighty degrees. You've really turned my life into an adventure. I thought I was happy and content before, but..." He pressed his lips together and shook his head. "Not anymore. I wasn't happy and content. Well, maybe I was. But not like now. Now my life is fulfilled."

Molly loved what he was saying to her, especially since he'd obviously had a speech in mind but was basically winging it at that point.

He turned his head and looked at their friends, who were watching with giddy smiles on their faces. "To Molly."

"To Molly." Everyone repeated the cheer.

"Let's sit down," Eddie murmured after they took a sip from their glasses. Molly hoped he didn't notice that she barely took in any of the drink and set it in front of her plate where it would sit for the rest of the night, never to be emptied or refilled.

Molly dug into her meal, trying hard to regulate herself so she wouldn't feel or look like a pig. But she couldn't help eating more than she should have. She was heavy with food by the end of it and ready to take a long nap.

Despite the urge to quit and go home, when Eddie asked if she wanted to "walk off the weight they'd just packed on," she couldn't resist saying yes. Walking was excellent exercise, she told herself.

She pulled her sweater around her as they walked into the breeze down the boardwalk. There were other people there. It wasn't their first walk together and it wouldn't be their last. Molly had already decided that. She was going to make it their spot. No matter that everyone else in Vinton enjoyed that particular area by a long stretch of water that wandered haplessly through the middle of the city, forcing the city developers to put in a lot of bridges.

Unlike the last time they'd walked that boardwalk when they'd first been showing interest in each other, now they were hand in hand. If she felt cold, he would warm her up. She could count on that.

They hadn't talked much about what she'd gone through the past few weeks while they'd been sharing dinner with their friends. It seemed like an unspoken decision between them all. They just wanted her to have a good time and eat after being starved for an entire day.

Molly was ready to talk about it, though. And she knew Eddie had found out more about the case with Teresa than she did. She knew full well Steven had been getting text updates as the evening went on. They had found Teresa, she knew that. What happened to the woman, she didn't know.

"I guess I'll have to testify, won't I?" she asked, crossing her arms in front of her and leaning over the railing.

"You might," Eddie replied. She knew he wouldn't need any explanation about what she was talking about. He understood. "But it won't be such a bad thing. You'll do fine. Thank goodness you didn't get... like hit or anything. Beaten. Assaulted."

She heard the tension in his voice when he talked about those awful things. She didn't want to think about it either. "Oh, I'm fully aware it could have been much worse for me. I feel blessed that Vinnie turned out to be caught up in something way over his head. Did Steven tell you if anything is going to happen to him?"

Eddie pulled in a breath through his nose. "Well," he replied, "Steven did say that the cops told him it was up to him if he wanted to press charges on Vinnie for digging up the land and stuff. But Steven isn't going to press charges. I'm pretty sure he's going to take care of Vinnie. The right way. He'll give him some of those gems so he can have some money, and I heard him discussing a new book deal."

Molly looked at Eddie, her eyebrows together. "Who? What? What book?"

Eddie chuckled. "I'm talking about Vinnie's book. The one his father published. That Steven found. He's going to have it republished with all the new information and have Vinnie's name put on it."

Molly was impressed. Steven always had the best ideas. It was nice because he had the money to put those ideas into action.

"Well, I'll be," she murmured. "That sounds amazing." She grinned at Eddie. "Think we'll get mentioned? We had something to do with this, too, you know."

Eddie raised his eyebrows. She could tell he was trying to be as serious as he could. "I mean, we'd have to be, wouldn't we? It was us that even told Steven about the treasure in the first place and then him and Jack are the ones who dug it up. We were there when it came out of the ground, so that kind of makes us part of the founding team, right?"

"Founding team?" She blinked at him.

"Finding team?" he suggested.

"Finding team?"

They laughed.

"I suppose you could say we are part of it all, too," she said when their laughter died down. "I've got plenty of space on my wall for a huge portrait of myself, beaming and holding up the new book with my name mentioned in it."

This made Eddie laugh again, much to Molly's satisfaction.

She beamed at him and scooted a little closer, enjoying the breeze that brushed past them and the fact that they were so close, it couldn't pass between them. She enjoyed feeling his body pressed against hers, keeping her warm. His arm was around her back. She laid her head to the side on his shoulder and discovered he was exactly the right height for her to do that.

Her heart jumped at that thought.

Maybe he was perfect for her after all.

Epilogue

Molly stood outside the Inn, looking up at it. On a normal day, she wouldn't have taken two seconds to stop and look up at the majestic building. But the new wing had been finished. And with the influx of money from the gems Steven found, he'd had the entire exterior reinforced. He'd had a new sign built to hang over the entrance. It was bigger and better than the other one, with swooping letters and a flashing LED ocean waves light above the words. It almost looked like literal waves were splashing over the sign.

Steven stood in front of the rest of them, his hands together, his voice booming over the small crowd. It wasn't just the gang there, though Andy had come back from North Carolina for the occasion. He was there with his wife and step-daughter. All the kitchen staff members who were able to attend were there. In fact, every member of staff that wanted to be there and could be there was standing outside the front of the Inn, taking up a good portion of the parking lot in that area.

There was a pleasant hum of voices in the air as everyone listened to Steven and responded to his words to each other. Molly heard no unhappy tones.

"There you are."

She smiled when Eddie came up behind her. She didn't even have to turn around. She knew it was him. He slid one arm around her shoulders and then she looked over at him with a warm smile of affection. "There *you* are," she repeated back to him.

"So I just wanted to thank you all for being here today so I can unveil the new Inn sign to you all. I know you're going to like it. I had a lot of help with the new designs and everything that you'll see inside. Wait till you see the employee break rooms. They've all got new and improved snack machines and everything. All departments have new coffee makers, those machines, so you can have any drink you want! Almost."

Laughter flitted through the crowd. Lots of calls of "thanks" and "best boss ever" filled the air. Then laughter again.

"Things are going to look better and better around here," Steven continued, speaking loudly enough for his voice to carry through the air. "If you see anything that is still missing, no matter how small, please let your head of department know, or me or one of the other heads of management, even if it isn't in your department. I've still got those cool, old-fashioned suggestion boxes around the Inn in various places. Leave your thoughts in there if you care to. No negative stuff. We don't do that here."

More laughter.

"I mean it, let's try to stay positive with our suggestions and thoughts. If there's anything you want to complain about, you can always come to me in my office. Anyway, thanks for being here and working with us here at the Inn and just remember that you're a valued member of our team and we wouldn't want you feeling any other way. So let us know what you think!"

He stepped aside, holding his arms outstretched toward the new entrance to the Inn as if he was showcasing something on display.

Eddie jogged Molly's elbow. "Did you get a new coffee maker? I didn't get one."

Molly grinned at him. "You have a little office, Eddie. No one cares about you in your little office."

Eddie looked hurt and Molly laughed, throwing her arms around his neck and showering his face with kisses. "You know I'm only joking. I care about you. I love you! That's why we're getting married next month."

"Do you think six months is long enough to court?" he asked.

She raised one eyebrow. "Court? What is this, the 1800's? You mean be engaged right? Besides, I thought courting was just another word for dating. And why would you even think of that word in the first place?"

He laughed. "I don't know. Came out of thin air. Sometimes I like to be retro."

Molly had to laugh with him. "Retro is 1970's, not 1800's. No one alive today lived in Victorian times."

Eddie opened his mouth but laughed and closed it again when Molly swatted at him.

"Don't you dare, Eddie Button. Don't you dare say the oldest person in the world did or something like that."

"I can think of some really, really old people who might possibly have lived that long ago."

"Oh, you!"

Eddie swept her off her feet and spun her in a small circle before putting her back down right in front of the rotating doors Steven had installed.

"Why thank you, kind sir," she said, tilting her head to the side. "I was hoping I could go through these doors to get in. I think they are so much fun."

"You must be a ball at roundabouts then."

Molly laughed. "Are you kidding? You're talking about involving a car on those. Fun to be had by all!"

Eddie chuckled. "I'm not sure about that. But hey, whatever floats your boat."

As Molly and Eddie joined the others in the concourse on the other side of the new entryway, Molly thought about how much things had changed in just the last six months. She'd been at the Inn for five years and nothing fun and adventurous had happened to her.

Then along came Eddie. Now her life was filled with love and happiness.

They might not be adventurous enough to go climbing Mount Everest, but Eddie was the perfect amount of fun for her. He liked to do the same things and have a good time the same way she did. She had yet to see him fully lose him temper. She'd seen him angry but not lose his temper.

She liked a man with a calm, level head.

"Molly?"

She reached out to stop Eddie from continuing forward when a woman said her name behind her. Both she and Eddie turned back to see a woman in a smart business suit holding out a big manila envelope to her.

"You wanted these sent to you as soon as they were done," the woman said. "But I thought I'd just come and bring them to you."

Molly's heart gave a little jump. She looked at Eddie, who seemed as excited as she was.

"Do you know what these are?" she asked.

"I think so," he replied, anxiously. "Open it and let's see."

Molly untied the cord around the back of the envelope and lifted the flap.

She reached in and pulled out the small stack of papers.

Holding the papers in the hand with the envelope, Molly rested her eyes on the beautiful invitation card she held before her. It was going to be a wonderful day.

The day she, under God's watchful eye, pledged to spend the rest of her life with her perfect man, Eddie Button.

***

Did you love this book? Then please help me by writing and posting a review. Thank you!

***

Sample of <u>Christmas Anel Joy</u>, Book 1, Three Christmas Angels Series by Morris Fenris:

Prologue

Guardian Angel School

Heaven

"Hallelujah! Amen!"

The sound of the voices faded away as everyone paused, serene smiles upon their faces.

"Very nice. Let's all take a few moments to ourselves before the celebration starts. Polish your halos. Fluff your wings.

Practice your smiles." The choirmaster smiled at them before leaving the room.

Matthias watched as the angels that were part of the angelic chorus departed the choir room, and then he frowned as three little white robed angels snuck out the side door. He was debating about following them when a voice spoke from behind him.

"I wouldn't waste any time going after them. Those three look like they're up to something. I thought this was supposed to be a celebration and yet, they look as if they are preparing for a funeral mass."

Matthias turned and nodded his head, "I was just thinking that same thing. I was hoping to have a quiet Christmas season, but with those three..."

"...there is no such thing as *quiet*."

Matthias nodded and then sighed before heading for the same door where the trio had made their escape. Alexander, the angel in charge of the guard, chuckled and then headed for the courtyard and his post for the rest of the day's celebration.

Rather than celebrating Christmas on December 25th only, Heaven celebrated for the entire month. Matthias looked forward to partaking in today's celebration, but first, he had three wayward angels to round up.

He watched the last of the trio slip around the hedge at the back of the school. Pausing beside a fountain on the other side of the courtyard, he kept his distance for the moment but made sure he had a clear view of them as they entered the building. Each of them took a seat at a small table, one dropping her head into her hands while the other two looked both morose and hopeless.

Hopeless? Guardian angels weren't allowed to look hopeless. No angels were allowed to ever look hopeless. There was no such thing within the Heavenly realms. Angels were supposed to inspire, bring about hope, and encourage humans to have faith; never give up or wallow in despair.

Sighing, Matthias stood to his full height and moved in their direction. It was time to fulfill his responsibilities. He was in charge of training the newer guardian angels. He entered the small schoolroom and then stopped a few feet away from the three.

"What are you three angels doing?" Matthias asked. "The celebration is about to begin."

When none of them offered an answer to his question, he crossed his arms over his chest and made a noise letting them know his patience wasn't everlasting.

Young angels in training could be considered quite troublesome by some of the older angels, but Matthias had willingly embraced taking the youngsters under his wings and helping them become the very best guardian angels they could be. This was his second year supervising this particular trio of angels. He knew better than to let them congregate and share their woes with one another. In the past, that had led to them giving one another advice, most of which violated the angel code and had forced him to intervene and correct the resulting situations. He did not look forward to repeating those experiences this Christmas season.

He cleared his throat to gain their attention and then met their eyes, one by one. "Well?"

"My little boy is so sad," Joy told him, dramatically tossing her hands out to her sides.

Joy was just beginning her second year of guardian angel training. She had struggled with several of her assignments in the past twelve months. In order to graduate from the guardian angel school, the little angels were given a variety of special assignments. All three of these angels had failed their special assignments the year before and were being given another chance to fulfill their duties without interfering in ways that were off-limits.

Humans were complex creatures with a God-given free will. While the angels could help facilitate opportunities, they weren't allowed to force or coerce their charges to do the prudent and correct thing. Joy had forgotten that fact the year before when she had played upon her charge's emotions in order to get them to follow a certain path. Unfortunately for Joy, human emotions were very volatile. Soon enough, her charge realized she had been manipulated but had blamed that fact upon a close family member, not where the blame had truly belonged—on her guardian angel.

Matthias had removed Joy from her guardianship of that human and had spent the next two months helping to bring about a reconciliation between the two humans; all because of the misconception that had arisen by Joy's overstep. Explaining the situation to the Archangel who oversaw the entire guardian angel program had been even worse. Matthias never wanted to go through that experience again.

Matthias nodded in acknowledgement of her response and then looked to the next angel. "And you, Hope? The last time we talked you were excited about your current assignment."

"My charge doesn't even want to celebrate Christmas this year," Hope stated, huffing out a breath, as she dropped her chin into her cupped hands. "How can anyone not want to celebrate Christmas? It's not...well, it's just not right. Or human. They love Christmas and their made-up celebratory figures. The snowman who danced and sang..."

"...and then melted when the sun came out," Matthias told her with a small smile.

"I'm talking about before that. And humans love the story of the little reindeer whose nose glowed and could fly. That story had a happy ending."

"But the idea behind Christmas has nothing to do with those things," Matthias reminded her needlessly.

"I know that." Hope nodded and added, "But my charge's file states that she loved all of those things until a year ago. Now, she abhors the very idea of Christmas. I'm trying not to hold that against her, but I must confess; it's very hard. Christmas is the most wonderful time of the year, but my charge hates it."

"Well, at least your charge doesn't visit the cemetery every day. It's really sad to watch her cry—day after day—and not even try to go on living her life," Charity added.

Charity was the most mature of the angels in training and had already successfully completed two of the three special assignments. If she was successful in helping her current charge overcome a soul-searing grief, she would graduate at the end of January.

Matthias looked at the three and shook his head, "So you three are just going to sit around up here moaning about your difficult situations rather than try to find a solution to them?"

Joy looked up at him. "What are we supposed to do? I mean, it's only a few weeks before Christmas. How are people supposed to remember they're celebrating the birth of the Christ Child if they are so unhappy?"

Matthias grinned. "You find a way to make them happy. Help them remember the good things in life and give them hope which is what Christmas is all about. Your job is to try to get your charges to see that. Remember...a guardian angel doesn't just keep their charge from getting run over as they cross the street; you also have to help your charge in the emotional, spiritual, and mental realm."

The three angels looked at each other. Their expressions slowly started to change. Hope was the first to speak.

"I could help Claire want to celebrate Christmas."

"And I could help Maddie find another outlet for her grief," added Charity. "What about you, Joy? Why is your little boy so sad?"

Joy was happy that her friends were coming up with solutions. Maybe they could help her brainstorm a solution to her little charge's request. While the other two angels had been assigned adult charges, Joy had been assigned to watch over a little boy. She'd considered herself the luckiest of the three when they'd been given their assignments. Now, she wasn't so sure. "My little boy wants his mama not to be so sad. She's lonely. He wants to help her but doesn't know how."

"Maybe she needs a puppy to love?" Hope suggested with a smile.

"Puppies are nice. So are kittens," Charity offered. "This time of year, there are always an abundance at the animal shelters. Maybe your little charge's mother could adopt a new pet?"

Joy appreciated their help, but she didn't think either of their answers were going to help Sam, her charge. Puppies and kittens took a lot of energy. After watching them, Sam's mother lacked extra energy at this time.

Matthias squatted down so that he was eye-level with the littlest of the three angels. "You'll find a way. I have faith in you."

"Thanks?" Joy queried, wishing she had as much faith in herself, as the head of the angel school seemed to have. "Maybe we should brainstorm more ideas..."

Matthias shook his head, "That is not going to happen while I'm around. I'm still recovering from the last brainstorming session you three had together. If you need to bounce ideas off of someone, I am always available to you."

Joy gave him a sheepish look and then snuck a glance at her two companions, noticing that they also looked embarrassed and were trying to avoid Matthias' searing glance. She decided it was up to her to put Matthias in a better mood. She offered him a small smile. "I guess I should probably get back down there, huh?"

"That would be a good place to start," Matthias agreed with a nod and warm smile. "You should all be busy trying to help your charges right now. Christmas is only two weeks away. You all should know better than anyone just how fast time can fly. Go and tend to your charges and remember; I am always here if you need advice or just to talk through a plan."

Hope, Charity and Joy nodded dutifully, and each said, "Thank you."

Matthias smiled at each of them. "Off with you all now. Go enjoy the celebration for a bit and then take that enthusiasm back to your duties. We'll have even more to celebrate once you three have your charges sorted out."

Joy looked at her friends. They all silently agreed. They were going to help their charges, whether those charges wanted to be helped right now or not. Their charges would never know why their situations had changed. The angels would have to comply with the rules and regulations for interactions with their humans. They would need to keep in mind; where there was a will, there was always a way.

Joy smiled and said, "I'm heading down there right now. Thanks, Matthias."

"What about the celebration?" Hope asked her, glancing out the window of the schoolroom to see the other angels gathering around the center of the courtyard. The choir performance was about to start.

Joy shook her head, smiling brightly as she replied, "There's so much to be thankful for and happy about this time of year. I don't need a celebration to remind me of that. I just need to figure out how to make Sam's dream come true. Then, everything will work out just fine."

Matthias smiled approvingly at her. "Good luck to you, Joy. I look forward to hearing a good report from you. Charity and Hope, good luck to you as well. The miracles of Christmas are just beginning."

Chapter 1

Two weeks before Christmas
Denver, Colorado

"Bye, Mrs. O'Toole," Sam waved as he skipped off the school bus.

"You go right up to your mother's office, Sam," the smiling bus driver told him.

"I will. I promise." Sam struggled for a moment to put his arms through his backpack straps. After a little hop, it settled into place. His winter hat had shifted only slightly atop his head of wheat-colored curls.

He rushed headlong for the double glass doors, not even breaking his stride when the security guard, Jim, saw him coming and held the door open.

"Good afternoon, Sam."

"Hi, Mr. Jim. I'm in a hurry."

"I can see that. Have a good afternoon."

"I will!" Sam yelled back.

He started for the bank of elevators, only to shake his head at the crowd already waiting for their turn in the foyer. He veered to his left, pushed through the door to the stairwell, and ran up the stairs until he reached the third-floor landing. He pulled open the heavy door that was stamped with a big red three. Sighing with relief, his feet hurried over the carpeted hallway as he headed for the office at the end.

Sam rushed into the office that had City of Denver, Planning and Events Division stenciled on the door. As always, his mother sat her desk. Sam was oblivious to the presence of his guardian angel, hovering just behind him, as she kept watch over her young charge. He was slightly out of breath, but that didn't dampen his enthusiasm one bit.

"Mom. I'm here. Can we go to the park now?" He wiggled his arms and allowed his backpack to drop with a dull thud to the floor.

Melissa Bartell looked up from the paper she'd been studying and forced a smile to her lips.

"Hey, little man. How was school?" She opened her arms and the little boy rushed into them, hugged her briefly, and then danced away again, unable to stay still for even a few seconds.

"School was good. Can we go now?" Sam asked, hopping from foot to foot and twirling toward the large windows in the office that overlooked the city below.

"You saw that it was snowing outside, right?" Melissa asked, as she got up from her desk and joined her son at the windows. When her cell phone beeped, reminding her that she was running late for a meeting, she reached for the coat she'd discarded an hour earlier. "Sure you want to go hang out in a city park covered in snow instead of at home where it's nice and warm?"

"Yeah." Sam rolled his eyes at the same time he nodded his head while adding, "I have my hat and my gloves." He held up the gloves and then waved his stocking hat in the air for her to see.

Melissa tousled his hair and then smiled down at him. "Okay, I guess I can stress while walking through the park as well as I can stress sitting here. Let's go."

Sam frowned at his mother's comments and Joy leaned closer, wondering what was bothering the beautiful young mother. It was easy to see where Sam got his coloring from, his mother's long blonde tresses had streaks of gold and a blonde that were so light they were a shimmery white mixed throughout. Her gray eyes matched Sam's, as did the small dimple that appeared in her cheek as it did in Sam's whenever he was happy and smiling; behaviors that happened far too seldom in recent days for Joy's liking.

"Why are you stressing?" Sam asked, taking his mother's gloved hand, as they left her office and took the elevator down to the ground floor. His mother nodded at Jim as they exited the building and began the short walk to the city park. There was a slight breeze, but Sam didn't even feel the cold. He was waiting on his mother for an answer to his question.

Melissa glanced down at him and made a silly face, "It's been a bad—very bad—day."

Sam pursed his lips at her reference to one of his favorite books, *Alexander and the Terrible, Horrible, No Good, Very Bad Day.*

He highly doubted his mother was capable of having such a day, but then again, being an adult seemed like lots of work and very little fun. He stepped a little closer to her and then nodded and pursed his lips in a bad imitation of the look she always gave him in such a situation. "So, tell me all about it."

Melissa chuckled and shook her head at his silliness. "Where have I heard that before?"

"You. It's what you always tell me when I've had a bad day. I'm all ears, Mom."

Melissa shook her head again and laid a hand on his jacketed shoulder, "Thanks, sweetie, but you don't need to worry about my problems."

"Mom! You always say we're a team of two." Sam danced away from her and turned around so that he was walking backwards and threw his arms out to the side. "You talk and I'll listen."

Melissa raised a brow at her son and then spun him around, so he wouldn't stumble and fall into the street. "I've heard that before, as well." She winked at him and then explained the most pressing issue on her mind. "So, I got a phone call earlier this afternoon. It seems there was an accident, and the Christmas trees aren't coming," she told him, keeping her eyes straight ahead. She tried to push aside the panic saying the words aloud had created.

A Christmas Festival without Christmas trees? Who had ever heard of such a thing? If the festival wasn't a success this year...People from all over the Denver area come to visit the festival with the intention of purchasing their Christmas tree at the end of the outing. Once word gets out that there are no Christmas trees this year, will anyone even bother to drive across town?

Sam stopped walking, pulling on his mother's hand to gain her attention. "The Christmas trees aren't coming? But...but the Christmas trees...you can't have a Christmas festival without Christmas trees."

Melissa nodded sadly and squatted down, so she was on eye-level with Sam. "I agree, buddy. However, this close to Christmas, there's not enough time to find another supplier to haul them out here. Besides, the two Christmas tree farms I called this afternoon don't have enough trees or manpower to harvest the trees they have left. I don't know what I'm going to do. I've kind of exhausted my available options."

Sam nodded, as Melissa stood back up, and they continued walking. His little expression was still far too serious, as they entered the park. Almost immediately, his mother was snagged by a vendor who had questions. Sam knew it would be quite a while before his mother made her way to the center tent and impatience won out.

"I'm going to the nativity scene, Mom," Sam called out even as he was walking away.

"Sam, stay where I can see you. Okay?" Melissa called out after him. The nativity scene was just a few dozen yards away from the event tent and easily seen from their present location.

"I will." Sam waved and took off, making sure he walked through the fresh snow and left his mark upon the landscape.

The city park where the festival was being held sat between the Museum of Natural History and the Denver Zoo. It was a large property and included a small golf course which was now closed due to the inclement weather. Melissa was only utilizing one small corner of the park for the Christmas Festival. In the distance, one could see the warning fence that had been erected to keep festival attendees from wandering onto the golf course.

The year before, a group of teenagers had wandered onto the golf course during the Christmas Festival and had vandalized the caddy shack before anyone had realized what was happening. The damages had been small, but the city manager had blamed Melissa for not having foreseen that such a thing might happen. Melissa had assured him that additional precautions would be taken this year. She could only cross her fingers as the opening of the festival neared and pray that they wouldn't have any incidences. Too much was riding on the festival being successful this year.

Melissa finally broke free from the vendors and headed for her makeshift headquarters here at City Park. Several large, pressurized domes had already been set up where vendors could sell their wares and where she and her staff would oversee and manage the festival. Hot air kept the domes inflated and also warmed the air inside, making them a pleasant escape from the chilly weather outside. This was a new amenity being offered this year. Melissa was hopeful it would bring more people out in attendance.

Her assistant met her with a stack of messages. Melissa inwardly cringed when she saw more than half of them were from the last man she wanted to deal with today. The city manager. She tucked the messages from him to the back of the pile, ignoring the knowing smile her assistant sent her way, and then headed for her makeshift desk. With any luck, she wouldn't have any more problems heaped on her shoulders. She needed a chance to figure out the tree situation and several other pressing concerns before she could handle even one more issue.

***

Sam reached the nativity scene and quickly slipped over the railing and sat down by the manger. This is where he'd been coming for the last week and, like those other times, he began speaking to the fake infant, telling it all about his mother's unhappiness and how he didn't need anything for Christmas; he just wanted his mother to be happy.

"Baby Jesus, Christmas is only a few weeks away. I don't need anything for myself, but please bring mama a husband. Maybe if she wasn't so lonely, she'd be happy again. I looked at school today, but I didn't find anyone who didn't already have a mama and a daddy. It makes mama sad when she comes to my school plays. She has to sit all by herself."

Sam grew quiet for a moment and then he added another request. "Mama's real sad about the Christmas trees. Could you maybe send her some of them, too? My friends all went and talked to the guy in the Santa suit at the mall, but I told them that was just silly. Mrs. Barnes taught us in Sunday school that Jesus has all the answers to our problems. That's why I'm talking to You about this."

He looked up at the winter sky and then glanced back at the plastic baby. "I know there's lots of people in the world with big problems, but maybe...if it's not too much to ask, you could answer mine?"

"Sam!" his mother's voice carried over the crisp air.

"I gotta go, but I'll be back tomorrow. Thanks for helping my mama." Sam got to his feet and climbed over the railing. He waved to his mother and rushed to where she was patiently waiting. When he reached her side, he announced, "I'm hungry."

She chuckled and nodded. "Tell me something new. How about we stop and grab a pizza before heading home?"

"Yes!" Sam agreed, as he raised a fist in the air. Pizza was his all-time favorite food.

***

Joy watched as mother and son headed for her vehicle, parked only a block away. A plan was already beginning to form for how to deal with Sam's unhappiness and his latest request. This was the first time Sam had actually mentioned what he thought might make his mama happy. A husband.

That immediately got Joy thinking. She was almost giddy at the idea of playing matchmaker. She'd have to follow the rules, which meant she couldn't toy with anyone's emotions. After last year's debacle, she'd promised Matthias to stick to the guardian angel code, but making sure Melissa Bartell had an opportunity to meet an eligible man wasn't in that book of codes. Melissa hadn't known that she should've been dreaming about a certain eligible man all these months.

Joy had been watching the request board which angels used to help one another do their jobs more efficiently. Just yesterday, a fellow angel had posted about her charge who was discouraged because he hadn't been able to find a buyer for his trees. The man had started his own Christmas tree farm a number of years earlier and was finally ready to start selling them, but a series of events had prevented him from harvesting them earlier. Now, he couldn't find anyone nearby to purchase them. The man's location was less than two hours away from Denver. To Joy, this situation was tailor-made in heaven. She wasn't about to let this opportunity slip away.

Joy immediately sent out a request and headed off to meet the other angel. To set things in motion, she needed a business card to fall into Sam's mom's hands. With the Christmas tree situation taken care of, now she only needed to find Sam's mom a husband. Compared to some of the other tasks she'd performed, this one should be a piece of cake...make that a Christmas yule log. It was the holiday season, after all.

Chapter 2

Two days later...

"Melissa, the guy from the tree farm is here," Sandy James called up the ladder to where her boss—the person in charge of making the Christmas Festival a success—was currently trying to untangle a string of lights. Why one of the city maintenance workers wasn't up on the ladder was unclear at the moment.

"Just a minute," a voice answered back, as the ladder started wobbling dangerously.

"Whoa!" Sandy lunged forward to stabilize the ladder just as another body pushed her out of the way and grabbed the ladder with big hands.

"I've got this," a deep tenor voice floated up to the top of the ladder. Melissa looked down into the bluest eyes she'd ever seen. "You okay up there?"

Melissa nodded and then blushed when she remembered he could only see the lower half of her since her head was partially concealed behind the festival's sign. Taking a calming breath, she called back down, "I'm fine. I'm coming down right now."

She descended the ladder, pausing when she reached the point where the stranger was holding it steady.

"Thank you," she murmured, as he stepped back, so she climbed the rest of the way down. She dusted off her hands and then looked past the stranger to where Sandy stood patiently waiting. She looked to Sandy's right and then gave the stranger a cursory glance. She wasn't sure who he was, but he was handsome, dressed in a red plaid flannel jacket with a hoodie pulled up over his hair. She briefly wondered what his hair looked like, but she quickly dismissed her wayward thoughts, bringing them back to the present. She didn't have time in her life for anything more than a fleeting second of appreciation for a handsome man—and this man definitely fit that category.

He appeared to be giving her appearance a thorough once-over as well. Melissa met his eyes briefly once more and then turned away, as she felt a blush creep into her cheeks. She didn't have time for...whatever, this was. There was no denying the man was gorgeous and exactly the type of man Melissa would be attracted to, if she ever gave herself permission to go down that road again. She currently didn't have time or the inclination for any sort of relationship if it didn't involve work and the festival. She most definitely didn't have time to nurse a broken heart. In her experience, heartbreak was the only thing at the end of the road when dealing with a handsome man. No, thank you.

She looked back at Sandy with a raised brow, "You said the guy from the tree farm was here. Where is he?"

She'd only spoken to the man on the phone a few times. She'd been expecting an older gentleman, possibly with greying or even white hair. His voice had been gravelly, and she'd pictured a slimmer version of Santa. Her imagination had placed him sitting in a rocking chair with a pipe in one hand, as he talked to her about his Christmas trees on the phone with the other. She didn't see anyone fitting that description nearby.

Sandy bit her bottom lip and then pointed unobtrusively at the stranger. Melissa turned her head and made eye contact with the handsome man. He nodded and stuck out his hand. She took it, ignoring how warm it was and how strong it felt.

"I would be the guy with the Christmas trees."

She ignored the way his deep blue eyes seemed to sparkle with mirth and forced herself to act professional. "Sorry. I'm Melissa Bartell, Community Events Director, and this is my assistant Sandy James. I was expecting..." She broke off, as she realized how rude her assumptions might seem if she were to give voice to them.

"Sandy and I already met," his deep voice reverberated inside her chest, and a feeling of warmth surrounded her. He shook her hand and the feeling of warmth flowed up her arm. "Jarod Gregory. Christmas Valley Pines." He looked around and then offered her a smile. "This is no small undertaking you have going on here."

Melissa smiled back, his comment helping her focus on the reason he was standing before her. "This is my fifth year running the festival. Each year, it seems to get more complicated than the last. Before I forget, thank you so much for stepping in at the last minute. The Christmas tree supplier we've used for the last few years hit a patch of ice coming through Idaho and their trailer overturned."

Jarod looked concerned. "Was anyone injured?"

"Only the four hundred trees he was carrying. Actually, I spoke to him a few days ago. He said quite a few of the trees remained undamaged, but his tractor trailer didn't fare as well. With it being so close to the holidays, he couldn't find another way to transport the trees out here until the twentieth of December which is a few days before the festival ends."

"Without the draw of the Christmas trees, we wouldn't get nearly as many people to attend the festival," Sandy interjected, moving forward into their small circle. "The city council is looking for ways to save money. This festival has been on their hatchet list for the last two years. If attendance was to suddenly drop, they would cut us out of next year's budget in a heartbeat."

Jarod nodded his understanding and then looked around for a moment before turning back to the conversation. "Well, I'm happy I could help."

"Let's go this way, and I'll show you what we have designated for the tree lot," Melissa told him, turning and walking toward the opposite side of the area cordoned off for the festival.

"This is actually the first year I've had trees to sell," Jarod informed her. "I inherited the land from my grandfather and moved out here from Oregon almost seven years ago now. My parents have a big tree farm back there and provided me the seedlings needed to start one here, but it takes years before a new operation is ready to do more than tend the trees." Jarod walked by her side, his long legs eating up the distance, but he walked at a leisurely pace, so Melissa was impressed that she never once felt as if she was having to hurry to keep up with him.

Melissa veered to her right and they began to cut across the center of the park. "Seven years is a long time to do nothing but watch trees grow. I had to admit I was actually shocked to find that there was someone in that area of the state who was growing trees. The pine beetles have all but decimated the national forests around here."

Jarod made a sound of agreement. "I noticed that when I first came out here. We have the same thing back in Oregon, so I was prepared for how to protect my farm. I spray the trees in early May and then make sure they're getting enough fertilizer and water throughout the growing season. Healthy trees don't seem to be the beetle's natural habitat, so I do my best to make sure mine are the healthiest in the county. So far, I haven't had any trees get infected."

"Well, I hope you don't. Let me show you where you'll be setting up. There's already a fence around the area with lights and such."

Melissa led him past the life-sized nativity scene, halting her forward progress when she spied her son inside the scene, kneeling next to the manger and the figure of baby Jesus. She saw his lips move, as he carried on a one-sided conversation with the infant and sighed. Sam had seemed so down this holiday season, and he'd been insistent on coming to the park with her each afternoon when school was out. He didn't seem interested in the exhibits being set up, except for one; the nativity scene.

Jarod nodded his head toward Sam and asked, "Someone you know?"

"My son," she told him with a small turn of her lips.

"He seems to be having quite the conversation over there," Jarod pointed out.

Melissa nodded, "A daily occurrence, I assure you." She stepped forward and called out, "Sam."

Her son turned his head and then waved. She waved back and gestured for him to join her, smiling when he picked up his backpack and ran to her. She bent down and hugged him when he got there, "Hey. I thought maybe you'd like to go see the Christmas trees."

Sam's eyes widened, and he looked at Jarod, "Did he bring them?"

Melissa nodded, "He did. On a big truck?" she guessed, looking to Jarod for confirmation.

"On a big truck. You look like you're pretty smart. You interested in helping me out for a little bit?" Jarod asked, earning a grin from Sam and a curious look from Melissa.

"What kind of help are we talking about?" Melissa asked.

"Well, I need to keep track of the trees as they're unloaded. I brought a couple of high school guys with me to get the stands on and everything unloaded, but I could sure use someone to help keep track of things. You can count, can't you?" Jarod asked with a smirk he barely managed to contain.

Sam stood up tall and nodded, "I can count really high. My teacher says I'm excst...excert...."

He looked at Melissa, and she provided the word he was looking for, "Exceptional."

Sam grinned, "Yeah. Exceptional. I'm exceptional at math."

"Great. You're the man I need."

Melissa shook her head as Sam took off sprinting across the snow-covered expanse of lawn, "I hope you know what you just signed up for."

"I have two nephews and three nieces," Jarod informed her. "I've missed them, and Sam seems like a great kid."

Melissa nodded, "He is."

They reached the fenced space, and she asked, "What do you think? Will this be enough room?"

Jarod looked around and then nodded. "Plenty. I'd better get things rolling here, so we can get unloaded before dark. Your assistant mentioned something about the festival opening a day early?"

Melissa gave him an apologetic look, "Yeah. Sorry I didn't have a chance to let you know. They're forecasting a big storm tomorrow and most of the vendors are ready to go so we're doing a soft open tonight. We'll open at six o'clock. Any chance you might be ready to sell trees by then? So many people wait to purchase their Christmas tree from the lot here...there'll be a lot of disappointed people if they have to go somewhere else."

Sam came running back to them, a giddy smile spread across his little face. "Mom! You should see all of the trees. Oodles and oodles of them."

"I hope so, we have oodles and oodles of people coming to buy them. About tonight?" she asked Jarod hesitantly.

"We'll be ready. After all, I have an exceptional counter ready to help out."

Jarod bumped gloved knuckles with Sam. She felt a pain in her heart. She'd married his father right out of college and had thought they were on the same page where their family was concerned. Sam's dad had left almost immediately after Melissa had told him he was going to be a father. He'd told her he wasn't ready to be tied down to a kid and, when she'd refused to even consider an abortion, he'd filed for a quick divorce and moved to California.

Melissa had been so excited about the prospect of becoming a mom, she hadn't even thought about fighting Tyler over the divorce or asking for child support. He'd made it clear he wanted nothing to do with his child. Melissa had petitioned the court to go back to using her maiden name. She'd given it to Sam when he was born and listed his father on the birth certificate, but that had been where Tyler Jamison's connection to her son ended.

As Sam had gotten older, she'd been struggling with a sense of guilt that he didn't have a man in his life to help guide him through the coming years. Sam was in second grade now. He was also the only child in his class that didn't have at least one father figure in his life. Her own parents were no longer around to help out. It was just her and Sam.

Some days, it was all she could do to get through the day by telling herself that tomorrow would be better. Tomorrow, she wouldn't feel lonely. Tomorrow, she'd find someone to confide in that didn't wear *Teenage Mutant Ninja Turtle* pajamas to bed. Tomorrow...

"Mom?" Sam was tugging on the hem of her coat.

"What?" she looked down and realized she'd let her mind drift. "Oh, Sam. I'm sorry. Lots of things on my mind this time of year. Are you okay sticking around and helping Mr. Gregory with the trees?"

"Sure. I count things really good."

"I know you do," she touched his shoulder for a brief moment and then took a step back. "I'll let you boys get to it, then. Sam, I'll be over at the event tent. When you're done helping Mr. Gregory, you come find me. Okay?"

"Okay," Sam readily agreed, dismissing her and starting up a conversation with Jarod right away.

Melissa watched for a long moment, pushing aside the guilt and unhappiness that always crept in whenever she thought of her fatherless son. She was doing the best she could, but the holidays were always hard. On both of them.

As she headed back to tackle the next item on her to-do list, she made a mental note to check out the local Boys and Girls Club right after the first of the year. Sam needed a male role model in his life. She'd heard from several people about the Big Brother program and how well it was doing. She couldn't make Sam's dad acknowledge his existence, but maybe she could find someone who would pay attention to Sam and help him grow into a fine young man. Someone who might be willing to teach him what being a real man was all about and answer the questions she knew he would have in the future but might not feel comfortable talking to her about.

"Sandy," she called out, as she entered the tent. "Did this evening's entertainment show up yet?"

"They just arrived."

Melissa nodded, glad that the local rock band had been willing and able to fill the stage on a moment's notice. They were popular amongst the younger population, and she was hoping that would draw a younger demographic out to the festival. "Anything else pressing right now?"

"You and a cup of hot chocolate," Sandy informed her, handing her a covered cup and turning her toward her makeshift office. "Go kick your feet up for five minutes."

"But..." Melissa took the cup and a few steps forward, but then she remembered the list of items she still needed to deal with.

"I promise none of your problems are going to go away in the next five minutes." Sandy gave her a look with one raised brow, daring her to argue. "You know I'm right."

"As always. Fine, but only for five minutes." She took the hot chocolate, sipping it as she sat down and leaned back in the chair. She tried to clear her brain, but that only allowed the image of the Christmas tree man to intrude. He was handsome...but she couldn't allow herself to be swayed by that. Nor could she spend time wondering why walking beside him had felt so...right.

Had I ever felt like that with Sam's dad?

Realizing where her thoughts were headed, she sat up and pushed the unfinished cup of hot chocolate away. No, she had a job to do. It was time to focus on the festival now. The past wasn't something she would change. The present day demanded she do her best to ensure the thousands of people who would be arriving later today had a memorable experience. Her personal problems would just have to wait.

***

You can grab a copy of this book at your favorite online retailer.

***

Oceanside Inn Series

Book 1: Love Came Just in Time

Thank You

Dear Reader,

Thank you for choosing to read my books out of the thousands that merit reading. I recognize that reading takes time and quietness, so I am grateful that you have designed your lives to allow for this enriching endeavor, whatever the book's title and subject.

Now more than ever before, reader reviews and social media play vital roles in helping individuals make their reading choices. If any of my books have moved you, inspired you, or educated you, please share your reactions with others by posting a review as well as via email, Facebook, Twitter, Goodreads,—or even old-fashioned face-to-face conversation! And when you receive my announcement of my new book, please pass it along. Thank you.

With profound gratitude, and with hope for your continued reading pleasure,

Morris Fenris

Self-Published Author

Did you love *All Things New Again*? Then you should read *Sara in Montana*[1] by Morris Fenris!

What happens when a California girl in the middle of a crisis meets a Montana guy?

Sara wished for a husband for Christmas this year and then married her boss. Now she is running for her life from him, with a warrant out for her arrest, and really needs a miracle to save her. To top off her week, she finds herself in the middle of a Montana snowstorm and sicker than she's ever been.

Trent quit the FBI to return home and became a sheriff. As the most eligible bachelor in Castle Peaks, he's had his share

1. https://books2read.com/u/mYGzgw

2. https://books2read.com/u/mYGzgw

of women chase him but has been disinterested; until now. He has a sworn duty to protect the town's citizens and assist other agencies in doing the same. When faced with a suspect in a criminal case, will he make the arrest or lead with his heart?

Join Sara Brownell as she runs for her life, straight into the waiting arms of local sheriff Trent Harding. Throw in a life-size nativity and plenty of snow, and watch the magic of Christmas come to life.

See how Sara forever changes the lives of Trent, as well as those around him.

Read more at https://www.facebook.com/AuthorMorrisFenris/.

Morris Fenris
Author

About the Author

With a lifelong love of reading and writing, Morris Fenris loves to let his imagination paint pictures in a wide variety of genres. His current book list includes everything from Christian romance, to an action-packed Western romance series, to inspirational and Christmas holiday romance.

His novels are filled with emotion, and while there is both heartbreak and humor, the stories are always uplifting.

Read more at https://www.facebook.com/AuthorMorrisFenris/.

44798714R00153